Turkish Delights

Trina Lane

About Turkish Delights

Three very different men from three different countries look to build a love greater than any Wonder of the World.

Project manager Garrett Sloan builds majestic hotels for the rich and famous around the world, but when it comes to love, all his relationships seem to crumble. His latest project lands him in Istanbul, where the desire he's held for a certain French architect heats under the Middle Eastern sun, and his resolve never to mix business with pleasure melts beneath the added fiery stare and skilled hands of a Turkish mason.

The three men discover they want to build a relationship to stand the test of time—much like Kyle LaFleure's buildings and Emir Şahin's stonework. As the bonds between Garrett and his partners grow stronger and more complex, they work to lay the perfect foundation on which to build a lasting relationship. Can the three men construct a relationship that will endure? Or will their love reach its zenith when their shared task of finishing the ultimate Ottoman luxury hotel reaches its completion?

Chapter One

G arrett glanced up from his laptop and looked around the business class cabin of the airplane. All seemed in order, but something had caught his attention. Then he saw out of the corner of his eye, one row back on the opposite side, a man had spilled his drink and was frantically trying to wipe the mess off his dress shirt.

Good luck, bloke. Hope you have a spare.

Garrett had learned the hard way to have a backup shirt and tie easily accessible when travelling for work. He turned his attention back to his laptop screen and re-started his music. He always had playlists ready for flights. There was nothing worse than listening to the incessant drone of jet engines—especially when he had this much work that needed to be done. He blinked a few times as the images on his screen blurred. A cup of tea would really be brilliant about now.

Garrett had checked in at Heathrow at five o'clock that morning for his flight at seven. Of course, that meant he'd actually left his flat in Epsom at four. Being a well-seasoned traveller, early or late flight times often appeared on his calender. However, because he only got two hours of sleep last night, he was completely knackered. Garrett's boss had called him to say that the officers and board of Totally Five Star Hotels, the company he worked for, had called a late meeting yesterday. They wanted to make significant changes to the design of their newest hotel in the thirteenth hour.

The flight from London to Istanbul was nearly half over, and while he would love to have a lie-down, there were simply too many items still on his checklist before landing. The newest property had a scheduled ground-breaking in a matter of a couple of weeks, and now he had to break the news of the changes to Kyle LaFleure, the primary architect on the project. Kyle had already been in transit to Istanbul when Garrett's boss had called the meeting. Garrett knew Kyle would not be happy. He'd already spent months drafting and finalising the blueprints for the hotel. They'd already got approval from the building inspector, municipality, infrastructure departments, and had obtained their building permits. Basically, they'd now have to start from scratch.

Garrett rubbed his temples as a headache threatened. He wasn't even sure if his boss's ideas were viable for the lot they'd purchased. He sensed many late nights working with Kyle in his future. That wouldn't necessarily be a bad thing, because Kyle was bloody gorgeous, but Garrett had a strict hands-off policy with co-workers. The last few months working with the Frenchman had significantly tested Garrett's resolve. It certainly didn't help matters he'd caught Kyle glancing in *his* direction on more than one occasion, either. Garrett jerked his head up quickly when someone touched his shoulder.

"Can I get you anything, sir?"

Garrett removed his ear buds. "A cup of tea? Please?"

The flight attendant walked off and Garrett dug a tiny bottle of painkillers from his laptop case—another thing he'd learned never to travel without. He placed the small capsules on his tray table, then looked back at his notes. The proposed changes were complex, but if possible, they would ensure that the new hotel would be the ultimate Ottoman luxury experience, which, of course, was the goal. Since being named the European Capital of Culture, Istanbul's popularity as a tourist destination had skyrocketed. Even with escalated tensions middle-east and a devastating earthquake crippling portions of the country. Istanbul maintained its status as a desirable location to visit and thrived as an urban epicentre of commerce. According to the demographics Garrett had gathered to prepare for the project, nearly twenty million visitors arrived each year—partially because of the city's historical draw, but increasingly because of its emergence as a major cultural and entertainment hub.

"Here you are, sir," the attendant said as she set his tea down.

"Thank you. I might just survive now."

He popped his painkillers and sighed as the warm brew fed stimulants to his veins. Garrett knew he had to have everything organised for his meeting with Kyle this afternoon, and with the pharmaceutical assistance, Garret should be able to get himself back on track.

Garrett gathered his carry-on and made his way off the plane. The local time was almost one in the afternoon. His meeting with Kyle was scheduled for three. Fortunately, his company had arranged for a car service to take him from Atatürk Airport to Beyoğlu. They'd also taken care of leasing a flat and a car since he'd be in Turkey for the duration of the project. He was supposed to pick up the car from the leasing office in the morning.

Garrett followed the signs to passport control for other nationalities after retrieving his checked luggage. He'd applied for his extended visit visa before leaving the UK. Since he'd already been to Turkey several times in preparation for the project, Garrett was familiar with which queues to enter. It seemed as if there was light traffic this afternoon, which was very relieving. He made his way up to the counter and handed over his documents to the agent. Garrett watched as the agent slowly entered his information into the computer system then stamped his passport without interest. He nodded his thanks, then retrieved his identification. He collected his luggage after checking the monitors for the proper carousel, then headed toward customs. Garrett didn't have to do a spot check, so he quickly entered the arrivals hall. He looked around for the car service driver. He'd been told there would be someone holding up a sign with his name on it, but it was hard to see through the hundreds of travellers dodging each other and toting luggage through the terminal. An older gentleman nearly collided with Garrett, but must have felt that the near accident was Garrett's fault, because he started waving his arms and cursing at him in Turkish. Garrett had picked up a few phrases on his previous trips and didn't appreciate the man's comments about his mother.

There was another bloke dressed in a black suit running toward the customs area. Garrett watched until the man skidded to a stop, looking around the terminal. He held up a sign and Garrett saw his name printed in large letters. He raised his hand as he walked toward the harried driver.

"I'm Mr. Sloan."

"My apologies for my lateness, sir. Your original driver was involved in an accident, and I'm a last-minute replacement. My name is Semih and I'm from Efendi Travel."

"No worries. I only just arrived. I hope the other driver didn't get hurt?"

Semih took the handle of Garrett's large suitcase and started walking. "No, no. More damage to the vehicle than him."

They exited the arrivals hall. As he stepped outside the glass doors, the natural air hit Garrett. After breathing the canned oxygen of the airplane, the freshness was a pleasant change. The temperature was probably hovering around twelve degrees centigrade, which was quite comfortable for March. Looking up into a blue sky was a pleasant change from the grey visage he was used to back home. Semih led him toward the area where a bunch of taxis waited. They reached a white Mercedes minivan and Semih opened the rear passenger door. Garrett stood by while Semih loaded his luggage, then climbed in.

"Can I offer you a refreshment?"

Garrett settled himself comfortably in the seat and looked out of the window. "No, thank you. The service gave you the address to my flat?"

"Yes, sir. I believe you are staying in Cihangir. That is a very nice neighbourhood. Lots of cafés and shops. Taksim Square, one of the most popular tourist destinations, is only a few minutes from there."

"Sounds good. My company made the arrangements, so I have no bloody idea what I'm walking into. Our build site is located right on the Bosphorus, so I hope it's nearby."

"Yes, sir. Very close. You are here for work?"

"Yes, I'm a project manager for Totally Five Star Hotels. We're building a new luxury hotel."

"There are many in Beyoğlu. What will make yours special?"

"You could transport so many of the choices on that side of the Golden Horn from here to any other Western European city, and the patrons wouldn't know the difference. They're full of modern furniture, minimalistic design and stark colours. Your city is full of rich cultural and historical significance, but travellers like modern and familiar conveniences. Our concept is to merge the two. Our hotel will be more than a place to stay. It will be an experience."

"I wish you success."

Garrett looked out of the window as Semih drove. The route they took was a new one to Garrett and ran alongside the Sea of Marmara. To his left was the city and to his right was an expansive green park with the waters just beyond. The motorway had a steady flow of traffic but fortunately wasn't too congested. Out on the water, personal craft and large ships alike dotted the slightly choppy surface. Garrett peered out of the window as they passed a massive sculpture. There were several hands holding up a bowl with what appeared to be fern leaves sticking out of the top.

"What is that?"

"I've heard it's supposed to signify people around the world supporting all life, but I don't know for certain. It just appeared one day. We are approaching the old walls of Constantinople. You can see the Yedikule Fortress outside your window."

Sure enough, looming stone walls appeared in the windows. There was greater traffic here, as it was a heavy tourist area, which allowed Garrett a better look. Since taking on the project, he'd done some reading on the region and had learned that initially the walls had surrounded the entire city of Constantinople. Throughout antiquity, there had been additions and modifications to the walls, and what stood today was a glimpse of the last great fortification system. Up ahead, he noticed something a little peculiar. It appeared that someone had literally cut the walls in half and built a motorway in the gap. If memory served him correctly, they were now in the area known as Fatih.

They turned away from the sea and toward the old city. Garrett gasped as the motorway passed right beneath the arches of an old Roman aqueduct. He didn't know if this was really the most efficient way to get to his new flat, but he appreciated Semih's personal tour of the city that would be Garrett's home for the foreseeable future. On all of his previous trips, he'd been in and out so quickly that he hadn't taken the time to visit all the sites he'd been reading about for the past two years. However, now maybe he would make the time, possibly even convince Kyle to go with him. Garrett was confident that he and Kyle could enjoy their time in Turkey without crossing any professional boundaries. At least he thought so.

"Mr. Sloan, if you look to your right, you can see the Süleymaniye Mosque. It is the biggest mosque in Istanbul."

"Wow, it's spectacular. I'm sure my business partner is already in love with your city. He's the architect of our crew and I know he's been itching to explore. Maybe I'll try to carve out some time to tag along with him."

"If I might suggest, sir, make the time. Istanbul is a city that will seduce you, given the chance. You seem like the type of man who would appreciate a true local experience. The tourist places draw the eye, but the heart of my city beats in the small bazaars, *hamams* and families who live here. May I suggest you contact my cousin, Derin? He runs a tour company and will take you to all the hidden gems. I will give you his information."

"Thank you. Maybe I will."

They came up to the Golden Horn, a waterway which served as a natural separation between the two divisions of the city. The area supposedly got its name because, during the Roman Empire, ships laden with gold sank beneath the waters of the Bosphorus inlet. One reason Totally Five Star Hotels had selected property along the coastline was because they loved the idea of playing off urban legend, not to mention the property values were some of the highest and most desirable in the city. Semih turned the vehicle onto the Galata Bridge.

"Do you know why this bridge is so famous?"

"I have a feeling you're not referring to the novel published a few years ago."

Semih scoffed. "No. Although I will admit it was an entertaining read. A bridge has existed across the Golden Horn since the sixth century. The Sultan Bayezid II even solicited plans for a design for one by Leonardo da Vinci in 1502, but that never came to be as the structure was a bit too ambitious for the times."

"Your kidding!"

"No, sir. We took inspiration for this modern design from the original Galata Bridge, built in the early 1900s. Unfortunately, a major fire destroyed it about thirty years ago. But back to my original question, the Galata is famous because it unifies the two identities of our city. On one side, you'll see traditional Istanbul, home to imperial palaces and religious institutions of the Ottoman Empire. On the other is the heart of Istanbul's entertainment and foreign merchant districts."

As soon as Semih spoke, Garrett recalled all he'd read about the bridge being romantically portrayed in literature as a pathway between two worlds. He thought it played off well with the design intent behind the hotel.

They'd reached the modern side of the city. Bigger, modern buildings now dominated the skyline. They passed by Taksim Square. At first, Totally Five Star had thought to build their hotel near there, but there were already several well-known luxury hotels in the immediate vicinity. Garrett had been the one to suggest staying in the Beyoğlu district, but finding a location that would be unique and still convenient for travellers. They knew their target demographics would be upscale tourists and business people working out of the financial district not far away. But to separate themselves from places such as the Marmara, Ritz-Carlton and InterContinental, they'd have to bring something special to the table. That's where the new design ideas came into play. And, frankly, *if* they could pull it off, Garrett thought they would have a gold mine on their hands.

They drove for only a few more minutes. Semih pulled to a stop in front of a building. Garrett looked down at his watch. They'd only been in the vehicle for a little over half an hour, but he felt as though he'd traversed both through time and over a great distance from one culture to another. Semih got out of the van and came around to open the passenger door. Garrett stepped out with his laptop case.

"I'll help you upstairs, Mr. Sloan."

"Thank you. That's very generous."

Garrett took his garment bag and Semih, the large piece of luggage. It wasn't a lot for the duration of his stay, but Garrett knew he'd be going back to London several times and could replenish his wardrobe as necessary. He appreciated the secure entry and noticed that the building seemed well maintained. There was a tiny lift, which just barely fit the two of them and the luggage. It was an old style with ornate iron bars through which Garrett could see the stairs. Five floors up, it came to a halt with only a slight bounce. Garrett pushed the gate away and peered at the door number across from the lift. He turned left and found the correct number at the end of the hallway. Using the key his office had provided before he'd left London, he opened the door to his temporary home.

The entryway was a narrow hallway. Garrett looked to his right and saw the bedroom. The rest of the living areas were to the left. They carried the luggage to the bedroom. Garrett removed his wallet from his trousers and removed several euros. He handed them to Semih.

Semih held up his hands. "Unnecessary."

Garrett offered again. "Please. You've gone way over and above the job description of a car service."

"Welcome to Istanbul, Mr. Sloan."

Garrett saw Semih out of the door, then explored the flat. He peered around the bedroom. There was a low platform bed, plenty big enough for himself and a partner. It took a few seconds to imagine himself and Kyle locked in each other's arms, rolling around the white sheets. Kyle's lithe form would arch in pleasure as Garrett sucked his cock. He shook his head to make the fantasy disappear. Best never to go there again—especially with Kyle's arrival in only a couple of hours. Their time together was hard enough on Garrett. How much worse would it be tonight, knowing that a perfectly good bed was right down the hall? He sighed and left the den of temptation. Outside the bedroom was a small alcove that served as a study. Across from the study was a door.

Garrett walked over and pulled it open. "Ah, good, the loo."

He stepped inside and relieved himself. As he washed his hands, he used the mirror that ran along the length of the wall to inspect the rest of the room. "Where's the...?"

Garrett shut off the tap, then turned around. There was no shower or bath. Out of the corner of his eye, he saw what appeared to be a removable showerhead attached to the wall. Upon closer inspection, he noticed a couple of small levers next to the nozzle. He looked down, found a drain in the floor, and discovered that there was a distinct slant to the concrete that would funnel water toward the drain. Garrett stood against the wall and activated the control. Above his head, water fell from the ceiling. Well, not really the ceiling. There was a plate filled with holes that allowed water to fall as though it were raining.

"Oh, that's bloody brilliant!"

He left the loo and went down the hallway. He found the closet that held a washer and dryer. The kitchen seemed well appointed and functional, the salon comfortable and stylish. The design of the whole place was very contemporary with clean lines, but the materials used were all warm woods and soft natural fabrics. There were floor-to-ceiling windows on every wall so far, which let in heaps of light.

Garrett opened one of the two sets of French windows. Stepping out onto the terrace, a stunning view of the Bosphorus rewarded him. "I've got to call Bridget at the office and give her a giant telephonic snog."

He left the windows open as he wandered about the flat. When he checked his watch, he realised that Kyle would arrive within an hour. He retrieved his laptop case and pulled out his work materials. He needed to get everything ready to drop the bomb on Kyle. Maybe he could soften the blow if he served him dinner—and several bottles of wine. Garrett headed for the kitchen to find out what kind of ammunition he had to work with.

Chapter Two

Kyle LaFleure stepped out of the taxi and looked up at the building in front of him. He tried to maintain his objective architect's eye, cataloging the features—four stories tall, four bays wide, cast stone cornices and mouldings. He'd date the building to mid-twentieth century. However, what had his heart beating erratically wasn't the display of architectural details of an era when buildings stood the test of time with quality materials and workmanship. No, it was the knowledge that inside that building was Garrett Sloan, the man who'd occupied Kyle's working hours and fantasies for the past year.

When Kyle's firm had won the bid for Totally Five Star Hotel's newest project, it had been a major coup. Then, to his shock, they selected him as the lead architect. This opportunity would be the greatest achievement of his career. Now, having worked closely with Garrett for the past year, Kyle knew he'd never again be the same man as he'd been before the tall Brit walked through his office door.

He let out a long breath and adjusted his satchel. At the entry door, there was a security panel. Kyle pressed the button for Garrett's flat. The screen came to life and Garrett's face appeared.

"You're right on time. I'm number four-A. Oh, by and by, the lift is a bit dodgy."

"I could use the exercise. See you in a few." Kyle heard a beep and the entry door unlocked. "Was he wearing an apron?" he said as he opened the front door and walked into the lobby.

Kyle jogged up the steps. By the time he got to the fourth floor, his heart raced, and he panted from the exertion. He really needed to get back to running regularly. Before he'd taken on this project, Kyle used to run a twenty-kilometre path along the Thames three times a week. He'd taken up running as a stress reliever shortly after moving to London and joining his firm. A colleague had told him it was a good way to clear his mind of all the interminable tasks on his agenda. At first, Kyle had been skeptical, but now he found that if he didn't run on a semi-regular basis, his body and mind got very agitated.

He stood in front of Garrett's door and took one last deep breath. Being a fully capable adult, he could control his urges around an attractive man. He and Garrett had been working closely for a little over a year, without stepping over any lines. There was no reason that they couldn't maintain the same discipline here. Besides, once they broke ground in a couple of weeks, Kyle would be far too busy to think about Garrett's tall, trim, athletic body. He wouldn't constantly fantasize about pinning Garrett to a mattress or desk, and most definitely not picture Garrett sucking his cock...

"*Merde!*" he whispered.

"Something wrong?" Garrett asked, as he opened the door.

Kyle cleared his throat and adjusted his satchel to shield his erection. "No, no. Just realised I forgot something."

Garrett held the door open. "Please, come in. I made supper because I fear we're going to be working late and not have time to eat out as we'd planned."

Kyle frowned as he walked inside. "What do you mean? Everything should be ready to go."

He followed Garrett down a short hallway. A round table with four chairs filled the space of the eating area in front of them. The table held an open laptop and had several papers spread all over the surface. It looked as if Garrett had been working for some time. Sheer curtains billowed from a breeze blowing through the open French windows beside the table. A fully stocked bar ran along the length of the exposed brick wall. He could use a stiff drink to calm him at this point.

Kyle peered around the column into the salon. A couple of low-backed couches flanked a square coffee table and a flat screen hung on the wall. Another set of open windows allowed fresh air into the flat. Kyle couldn't resist the allure of the terrace he spied outside. He set his bag on one chair, then stepped out.

"Nice view!"

"Yeah. Bridget really outdid herself by arranging the leasehold on this place," Garrett said while handing Kyle a glass of wine.

Kyle tried not to shiver at the sound of Garrett's deep voice behind him. He gladly accepted the glass and took a healthy swallow. He felt the warmth of Garrett's body. Their arms brushed as Garrett moved past him, and Kyle realised it was the first time they'd shared more than a professional handshake.

"I hope you like *sarma* and *baklava*. I made local dishes to initiate ourselves properly to the country.

Kyle turned and looked at Garrett. The man wore casual clothing—another first. The top couple of buttons were open on Garrett's tailored shirt, giving Kyle a tantalising glimpse of the base of the man's muscular neck. Kyle followed the trail of buttons down Garrett's flat stomach. The slacks hugged Garrett's hips, and the fit emphasised the man's lean build. He smiled as he realised Garrett was barefoot. How unfair was it that the man even had sexy feet?

"I've never had it. But as long as there's no shellfish involved, I'm all for trying new things."

"Then we should be fine. I found the recipe online. They're stuffed grape leaves, filled with rice, seasonings and ground meat. It took me a few tries to get the leaves to roll correctly, but I think they turned out properly. I have some yogurt to serve with them. I was thinking we could eat out here on the terrace."

Kyle glanced at the small table set for two. It looked cosy and even a little romantic, with the Bosphorus in the background. *Too bad it isn't a real seduction.* "That's fine, but I have to say I'm thinking more about why we have a lot of work ahead of us tonight instead of filling my stomach. What's going on, Garrett?"

Garrett sighed and set his glass of wine on the iron table. "There's been a change of plans."

He felt the blood drain from his face and his chest tightened. "What do you mean?"

Garrett took several steps toward Kyle and put his hand on Kyle's shoulder. "I know how hard you've worked on these plans—how hard we've worked for the past year on this project. Yesterday, I was called into the CEO's office and told that he wants to modify the design—and I'm not just talking about the curtains and bedspreads. It's going to require a complete rework of certain structural elements."

He reared back, very grateful for the balcony railing that kept him from falling to the street below. "What?" he exclaimed. *"C'est impossible! Ce que ces idiots mère putain ont une idée de ce qui se passe dans l'élaboration des plans? Pensent-ils que je viens gribouillé le dessin sur une serviette un après-midi?"*

"I know. I know. My apologies. But this was a decision above my head. Look, let's eat, then I can go over the details. We'll make this happen and it will be brilliant."

Kyle turned and braced his hands on the railing. It was a good thing Garrett knew French, because Kyle had a tendency to switch back to his first language when he was upset—or aroused. He winced as he realised he'd called the CEO of Garrett's company—who was paying Kyle's company a very impressive amount of money for their work—a mother-fucking idiot.

He studied the surrounding buildings, cataloging all the architectural details to calm himself. The Cihangir neighbourhood was a unique blend of historic buildings nestled among modern structures. Across the street was a stone, flat-roofed building with ornate cornices and friezes, while just down the block stood an ultra-modern glass structure.

Out of the corner of his eye, he watched Garrett set plates on the table, along with a bottle of wine. He turned and faced Garrett. "How bad? I will not enjoy this meal you've made if I'm panicking about throwing out a year's worth of work."

Garrett pulled out one of the two chairs and gestured for Kyle to sit. "I will not lie. This is going to be a challenge, but I have every faith in you."

He sat, and Garrett gave Kyle's shoulders a squeeze. He kept his eye on Garrett as the man leisurely strolled over to the other side of the table and sat as if he hadn't a care in the world. Garrett lifted the napkin and placed it across his lap. Kyle watched all the movement with a dispassionate gaze. So much work. So many hours spent hunched over his drafting table, and nearly getting carpel tunnel reworking blueprints on his computer until they were perfect—gone.

And he's sitting there looking at me as if it's no big catastrophe!

Kyle looked down at his plate where Garrett had placed several of the *sarmas*. There was a small dish of yogurt on the table. Garrett had put in a lot of effort to make this meal nice. The changes were obviously not his idea, so Kyle wasn't upset with him, but it still aggravated him to the point of fury that the corporate owner—who consequently knew nothing about structural engineering or architecture or any of the multitude of elements that had to be orchestrated for a project of this size to be successful—wanted to stick his hands in and swirl them around to make a big mess at this stage of the game. They'd had plenty of time to give their input during the initial planning stages. They had run all designs past them for approval, but clearly, the fickle rich felt as though disrupting the building schedule completely to satisfy their whims was no big deal.

"You're not eating?"

Kyle looked over at a frowning Garrett. He picked up a *sarma* and tried to smile. "I'm sorry." He took a bite. It was delicious, even if it went down his throat and lodged in his stomach like his *mémé's* duck mousse pâté. "It's good. Thank you."

A drop of wine lingered on Garrett's lips before he dabbed it away with his napkin. Kyle couldn't help but wish it was the man's tongue that had done the job—or better yet, his own. He really shouldn't be thinking of sex right now, but at least it kept his mind off the enormity of the work ahead of them.

"I'm glad you like them. I understand you being upset and distracted, but let's try to enjoy our meal. Then we can worry about what needs to be done."

He nodded. "How was your flight this morning?"

"Smooth, which is all we can ever hope for, right? And yours?"

"Ah, well, I visited my parents in Lyon for the weekend before coming here. My flight should have been only just over three hours, but because of a maintenance issue with the plane, it took me almost twice that time."

"Well, I'm one to believe that it's better to discover a problem with the plane while it's still on the ground and not in the air."

"True. Then things went smoothly. I will say your flat is much nicer than mine is. I love the modern design."

Garrett nodded. "I've only been here a few hours, but it feels very comfortable. I love all the windows and this terrace. The proper test will be tonight when I climb into that enormous bed."

"Hmm, too much space to roll around can make it difficult to get a good rest."

"Too bad I won't have someone to share it with me. Then we could help each other sleep, preferably after wearing ourselves out."

Kyle gasped in a lungful of air and choked. He coughed until his eyes watered. Garrett stood immediately and knelt in front of him, patting him on the back. Kyle caught his breath. He looked into Garrett's green eyes. In their emerald depths, Kyle thought he saw desire mingling with concern. He leaned forward a couple of inches. Garrett rested his hands on his knees, the warmth of his touch burning Kyle's skin through his trousers. Their gazes locked. Garrett tightened his fingers fractionally on Kyle's knees. Then Garrett closed his eyes and let out a long breath. It was as if the shutter of a camera lens had clicked and the moment captured moved forward. Garrett stood and took several steps backward.

He cleared his throat. "I'll go get the dessert."

Kyle stood and picked up his now empty plate. "I'm full. How about we get to work, and maybe we can have dessert later." Kyle gathered Garrett's dishes as well and carried them to the man, who still stood just outside the windows leading to the table where he'd dropped his bag. Garrett's gaze appeared trained on Kyle's lips and he resisted the urge to lick them.

"I'll grab the glasses and bottle," he said as he passed Kyle.

Kyle swore he heard Garrett mumble something under his breath that sounded like 'or several bottles'. He took the dishes into the kitchen that was just off the salon. The modern décor continued in there with stainless-steel countertops and appliances, mixing with warm cherry wood cabinetry. The appliances were small, about half the size someone would find in a normal house, but filled the space available with just the right balance. Kyle set the dishes in the sink, then crossed through the rectangular columns back over to the table.

He opened his bag and took out his laptop and a notepad. Writing longhand always helped him think more clearly. Plus this way he could study the blueprints on the screen and take notes without having to flip to another document.

"I'm ready."

Garrett sat and brought his laptop out of sleep mode. "Here's a list of the changes." He turned his screen around and showed Kyle.

Kyle felt his eyes bulge as he read down the list. Some requests were more interior design orientated, but others would require a complete overhaul of key structural elements.

"They want to convert the spa into an authentic *hamam*?"

Garrett nodded. "The idea is to bring a taste of the old city into the European side."

Kyle frowned. "Why? If someone wants old city Istanbul, they can simply make a reservation over there." He started scribbling down all the points on the list.

"Why do people want to stay in Taksim Square? What draws them to places like the Marmara and the Intercontinental?"

"Convenience and luxury," Kyle answered as he wrote. He made a notation next to the request for mosaic tiles in the baths.

"Right, and both places have a predominantly contemporary design—as do most of the hotels on this side of the city. So tourists and businessmen stay here, because it's familiar and comfortable, but then they travel over to the old city because they want to experience traditional Istanbul. They Google the best *hamams*, mosques and bazaars. The plan is to bring the exotic nature of Ottoman era Istanbul to the luxury and convenience of Beyoğlu."

Kyle sighed and looked down at the list. "I can understand the concept, but why at this stage? We're scheduled to break ground in two weeks! This is going to delay everything. We're going to have to get plans re-approved by the building inspector and the municipality. Get new building permits. That alone is going to cause at least two months of delay, not even counting the time I take to draw up new blueprints."

"I know."

"There's no way to change their minds?"

Garrett shook his head and held out the plate of *baklava*.

Kyle accepted the sweet consolation prize, took a bite, and sighed. "I'm going to have to videoconference with the firm and get the all the engineers' input once I talk to your boss and get a new wishlist and set of priorities. Find out exactly what they want to showcase. If they want a real *hamam*, then a complete redesign of the lower level will be required. That means we're going to have to adjust the guestrooms that were originally supposed to be on the second level. In fact, right now I'm thinking that we might want to revisit the possibility of using a single story design and bring in historical elements of the great

Ottoman designers such as Mimar Sinan. Any idea what we're going to do for a mason? Our contractors lack the experience to complete the projects I see listed here successfully.

"Actually, one of the first things I did after learning about the change orders was to source out a local expert. There's a man by the name of Emir Şahin who comes highly recommended. He's independent, and when I contacted him, he provided several quality examples of his work and references."

"Which, of course, you vetted."

"Absolutely. I have a concern about whether he can handle a project of this scope alone. Granted, ours is a boutique hotel, but we still plan to have thirty guest suites, not to mention the new *hamam*, restaurant, and common areas."

Quickly, Kyle looked up from his laptop. "He doesn't work with a crew?"

Garrett shook his head. "He's an artist who specialises in hand-carved stone. The samples he sent me included fountains, columns, fireplace surrounds and similar projects." He turned the screen back toward Kyle and showed him the images Emir had sent.

"Those are beautiful. I suppose a lot of the projects will require casting, but if they want the hotel to have an authentic Ottoman feel, hand carving will be required. Maybe the interior designer can find some architectural salvage items?"

"They want the hotel to be the ultimate Ottoman luxury experience."

Chapter Three

Garrett wandered through the grand bazaar. He'd come here once a week for the past three months and still had seen only a fraction of the five thousand shops. Today, he was on a mission to find a birthday gift for his mom. He'd heard there was a stall somewhere near the high-dome hall that had mother-of-pearl mirrors. Since his arrival in Istanbul, he'd done a little travelling. While on his adventures, he'd purchased several things for himself—a couple of ceramic pieces in Kütahya and three rugs from reputable dealers in Cappadocia. Garrett had even bought a stunning stained-glass lantern from the spice market right in Istanbul—although the bazaars were typically tourist traps. The flat definitely felt a bit more like home, but it was going to cost him a fortune to ship everything back to England once his time in Turkey ended.

The last three months hadn't been all one big holiday. On the contrary, after investing long hours in re-planning and logistics, they were ready to break ground on the Beyoğlu Ottoman Boutique once again. Personally, Garrett felt that if Kyle didn't get some kind of award for the new design, then there was no justice in the world. The plans were truly a work of art. A perfect blend of old world and new, which was the embodiment of the city. They had shifted the layout from two stories to one, but with the addition of the domes, stone and mosaic work, they weren't saving any money on building costs, not to mention the money they'd already lost by delaying construction. However, the owners had said repeatedly to 'spare no expense'.

Conflicts with the new schedule forced Garrett to seek new bids for the construction. He and Kyle had flown back to London on two occasions to get approvals for the working plans from the officers and the board of Garrett's company. The interior designer at Kyle's firm had said that he didn't feel comfortable in the new style, so Garrett had interviewed and arranged for one based out of Istanbul. Most of the subcontractors had remained the same, except for adding Emir to the payroll.

Emir Şahin. Bloody hell, even thinking his name had Garrett's heart racing a little faster. He'd been struggling enough to resist his attraction to Kyle, but fate was a cruel bint to tempt Garrett with not one, but two unobtainable men who consumed Garrett's fantasies. He'd lost count of how many nights he'd lain in his bed imagining himself and Kyle, and himself and Emir—and on several especially desperate evenings imagining all three of their slick bodies twisting erotically on the sheets.

He wove his way amidst the throngs of people. Touts called out to tourists aggressively, luring them to their wares. Garrett's gaze followed the blue, white and red mosaics highlighting the sweeping curves of the arched roof. Stalls filled to the brim with merchandise twinkled, beckoning shoppers to spend their money on 'one-of-a-kind' items.

He winced as an obvious tourist with brightly coloured Western clothing and an overly loud voice tried to haggle with a vendor. Haggling was a time-honoured tradition in the bazaar, but this man's skills needed much improvement. The gentleman walked away with his prize, holding it up over his head like some kind of trophy. While the display was more boisterous than Garrett would ever imagine himself doing, he appreciated the shopper's exuberance for the complete experience, regardless of the fact that he'd probably just bought a knock-off from China and had still paid too much money.

Garrett tried to make sure that all his purchases were genuine Turkish artifacts. He'd not bought any of his souvenirs here at the bazaar for that very reason, but he still loved coming here for the atmosphere. He had shown the carpets he'd purchased to Emir to get his opinion. The man had studied the weave and symbols, declaring them to be authentic and of good quality. Garrett saw a spice shop up ahead and wanted to pick up some curry for the supper he planned to make later in the week. Garrett stood in front of the stall filled with spices and seasonings, the air resplendent with mixing scents. He located the curry and almost gasped at the price. Forty lira for one kilogram was ridiculous! He'd gone to the spice market in the Fatih district two weeks ago and bought some for ten. He looked up at the shop owner and frowned.

"*On lira,*" he said, pointing to the Indian curry.

The stall owner shook his head vehemently. "*Otuz.*"

Thirty? Was the guy serious? Garrett knew he didn't look like a local, but he wasn't a total plonker. Garrett's Turkish had continued to improve in the last three months, but he was still far from fluent.

"*On beş ve daha fazla.*" He wasn't paying anything over fifteen. The vendor could kiss his arse. He'd find his spices elsewhere.

"You're still overpaying. If it's curry you want, I can show you a local market with the very best ingredients and respectable prices."

Garrett stiffened at the deep voice behind him. The same voice had haunted his dreams since nearly the first night he'd met the man three months ago. He turned to look at Emir—hypnotic inky eyes with the slightest Asian tilt, wavy coal-coloured hair, high cheekbones, currently framed by a two-day growth beard—and a smile that could brighten the darkest room.

"I know, but at least it's better than the forty he's asking."

Emir hummed. "Have you tested it? The turnover is not very high here. This may be weeks old and the open air does it no good."

He shook his head. "No, I hadn't thought of that. I'm still not used to buying spices from vendors. At home, they come in small sealed jars."

Emir stepped up to the shelf. *"Köri ne taze? Bana yalan söylemez. Arkadaşım farkı bilmiyor olabilir, ama ben yapmak size garanti."*

"Neden ilgileniyorsun ne bu adam satın alır? O talaş başka bir şey hak ediyor. Muhtemelen zaten farkı anlayamadı."

He had no idea what Emir and the vendor were saying to each other, but Emir's face suddenly darkened and he grabbed Garrett's hand, pulling him away from the spice shop.

"Emir?" Garrett tugged his hand out of the mason's grip.

They stopped in the middle of the walkway. Emir turned and looked back at Garrett, frowning. "The man was a *serrefsiz*. He does not deserve your money."

Garrett smiled and noticed that Emir's gaze lingered on his lips. "Thank you. I don't suppose you know anything about antique mirrors?"

"Want to look at your pretty face more often?"

"My mother's birthday. I thought I might find her a nice hand mirror as a gift."

"Here? Maybe in the central old bazaar. Come. I will take you."

Garrett followed Emir, surreptitiously watching the man's arse as he made his way through the crowd. Emir honed his body with years of lifting heavy stones, and Garrett appreciated the results. The masculine sway of his hips lured Garrett's gaze, although Garrett wasn't sure which was better—Emir's arse or the breadth of his shoulders. Those strong curves practically begged to have Garrett gripping them as Emir stuffed Garrett to within an inch of his life.

They crossed under an arch with an enormous neon sign labelling it as the old bazaar. He couldn't help but think that neon in a historical marketplace thousands of years old made the place seem a little disingenuous. He had little hope of finding an authentic antique here, but his mum didn't care about that. She simply liked pretty things, so Garrett would find her one. They came to a stall selling old weapons. Garrett was ready to move on, but Emir seemed fascinated by a sword.

Emir spoke with the vendor. His expression turned into one of pure excitement when the vendor allowed Emir to hold the weapon. Garrett took a step closer. The piece had some nice silverwork on both the blade and the hilt. Some kind of black wood made up the hilt. Emir handed the sword back to the vender, then turned toward Garrett.

"I've always wanted a symbol of my ancestors. That was a late nineteenth century *yatağan* sabre."

Garrett looked over his shoulder at the stall as they walked away. "Genuine?"

Emir nodded. "Not an antiquity of museum quality, but very nice. He wanted forty-six hundred."

He whistled softly. Maybe there were genuine antiques here. As much as he loved his mum, he wasn't spending that kind of money.

He was about to tell Emir that very thing when his companion put his hand on Garrett's back, steering him to the left. In front of them hung all matters of jewellery and various personal items. There were lots of items, including a lot of silver.

"I've bought things from this man for my sister before. He is deserving of your money, but don't worry, I won't let him rob you."

Garrett let his gaze roam the stall, not really focusing on anything yet. It was overwhelming to be truthful. So much silver. Some with inlaid stone and some with tremendous filigree in its own right.

"Arkadaşım annesi için bir ayna istiyorum." Emir looked over at Garrett. "I told him you were looking for a mirror for your mother."

The vendor smiled and held up his finger. Within a moment, he placed two compacts and a hand mirror in front of Garrett. All three were beautiful, but one immediately stood out for him. The back of the hand mirror had layers of geometric stars radiating from its centre. Garrett looked up at the vendor and gestured to the mirror. *"Ii tutabilir?"*

Emir picked up the mirror and handed it to Garrett. "Of course, you hold it. Back here, it is considered rude not to inspect a piece before purchasing."

The mirror had a wooden frame, possibly walnut, but the comprised embellishments of inlaid mother-of-pearl, tortoiseshell, and... Garrett examined it a little closer.

He glanced over at Emir. "What is this material?" He pointed to one of the inner rings.

Emir spoke with the vender quickly, then glanced back at Garrett. "It's green-stained ivory."

Garrett turned the mirror over to inspect the glass side. There were some mother-of-pearl inlays on this side as well. Some of the substrate on the glass had flaked off, and the glass was slightly cloudy, which probably indicated that it was the original material. That only added to the appeal in Garrett's opinion. The big question was—would he be able to afford it?

"Ne kadar?"

Garrett listened as Emir and the vendor spoke back and forth. He could tell by Emir's inflections and the couple of words he'd learned that they were haggling. He'd let Emir handle it since the man said he'd shopped here before. Garrett was trying very hard not to become attached to the mirror. He didn't want the vendor to see just how much he wanted the antique, but also if there was no way he could afford it, he didn't want to get his hopes up. He tried to appear casual as he glanced around the rest of the pieces on display. There were lots of necklaces, rings and bracelets—and a few teapots and some other thingamabobs, too.

Emir tapped Garrett on the shoulder. "I've talked him down to five hundred."

Garrett did a quick calculation in his head to convert the amount to euro. It was just over one hundred thirty. Not cheap, but he'd actually been expecting worse. And since his mum was turning seventy, she deserved a special gift. After all, she had given birth to him and had raised him—which she took great delight in reminding him of on multiple occasions.

Emir pulled Garrett aside. "If you like the mirror, I suggest you take him up on the offer. It's a good deal for a quality piece."

Garrett nodded to the vendor. The man rewarded him with a big smile, picked up the mirror and began to wrap it, then he placed it in a box. Garrett appreciated the extra effort. After paying the vendor in cash—it was the only way to shop in bazaars—Garrett and Emir walked away.

"Would you like to get something to drink? My treat, since you were such a big help."

Emir shook his head and Garrett swore that the dejection physically hurt.

"It is Ramazan—a month of fasting and prayer. I do not eat or drink anything from sunrise to sunset. But it will not offend me if you choose to do so in my presence. I know of a nice little teahouse not far that serves wonderful Turkish tea. It remains open because of tourists."

"Of course. I apologise. Not sure how I forgot since I neglected to put my earplugs in last night, and the drummer woke me at three o'clock this morning for *sahur*."

Emir chuckled. "Yes, they are good at that. Have you sampled one of our early morning meals yet?"

Garrett shook his head as he followed Emir. "No, I know the restaurant near my flat has a special banquet available, but I'm too attached to my bed to venture out and sample the offerings."

The two of them wove through the streets for several blocks with Emir beside him, talking about some of the history of the area and insider knowledge about the small shops. When they entered the outdoor teahouse, Emir claimed a table for them.

"You will have to stay up late then. Many of us rest during the day so we can partake of the night-time celebrations. You are in a city rich with the history of Islam during the holiest of months. It would be a shame not to experience it to the fullest."

Garrett adjusted his position on the low couch. The weather was perfect for sitting outside. Carpets hung all over the walls and draped over furniture. A little courtyard between two buildings housed the teahouse. A server appeared and placed a cup of tea on the low table in front of him. Garrett reached for the small cup and took a sip.

"Brilliant. You're right. I should get out before everything ends. Possibly in the next couple of days. Once we break ground next week, things will be quite hectic."

"My friend, the ending celebration, Eid al-Fitr, is this night. If you wish to go out, now is the time. I will be your guide, if you wish."

Is he asking me out on a date? No, not possible.

Garrett turned to look at Emir. Except for the tilt to his eyes, his features were very Roman. Since half the city technically lived in Asia and the rest in Europe, it wasn't unusual to see a blend of traits in natives of Istanbul. Not to mention the thousands of years of merging genetics as nations warred and settled the territory over and over. Emir, in Garrett's opinion, carried each one of his traits very well.

"You would do that for me? I admit, I'm partially afraid that I would get swept away in the crowds and hopelessly turned around in some back alley."

Emir scooted an inch closer and put his arm over the back of the sofa. "I would let nothing happen to you. And I can show you the heart of our city during this special time."

"Thank you. Would it be an imposition if I invited Kyle?"

Emir stiffened and frowned. "No, I did not realise the two of you…"

"Oh, we're not! Not that he's not… Or that I…" He cleared his throat. "Anyway, I just thought since this was his first time, too, it would be fun for us both."

Emir smirked. "Well, I do enjoy sharing a man's first time. However, I've never done it with two before," he whispered.

Garrett choked on his sip of tea. He tried to put the cup and saucer down without breaking the delicate china while he coughed. Garrett got himself under control then eyed Emir. Although there was a tinge of concern, the man's obsidian eyes glimmered with humor.

"You are the devil himself."

"I do not believe that I am evil, but I'd love to tempt you."

Garrett's breath caught, and the teacup rattled on the saucer. There was no mistaking that come-on. And, if Garrett didn't have to work with the man on the hotel, he would take Emir up on the offer in a heartbeat. But Garrett had developed his rules for a reason.

"And if you didn't work for me, I'd let you," he said, quietly.

"Then I will quit."

Garrett shook his head. "I need your talents to make this project successful. You are the only mason I interviewed with the skills to pull this off."

"So, must we sacrifice our desires in the name of commerce? I dislike this." Emir looked at his watch, then stood. "I would like to change your mind, but I must leave. It will be time for prayers soon. I will call you later."

Garrett stood and watched as Emir left the teahouse. He picked up the box containing his mother's mirror. Garrett left the teahouse and headed toward the tram station. The tram became his preferred mode of transport on his various excursions after a couple of very unpleasant taxi rides. He only used the vehicle his company arranged for him to have for day trips beyond the city, because driving in Istanbul was akin to working as an acrobat in a circus placed in the middle of the jungle.

He'd go back to his flat and review what needed to be done before the excavation crew arrived next week. Garrett expected Kyle to arrive back in the city tonight. He'd spent the last week in Lyon with his family. Garrett found he'd frequently picked up his phone to chat with the Frenchman, only to reconsider so not to be a nuisance.

They'd been in a meeting with the gaffer of the construction crew when Kyle received a call from his mother informing him Kyle's father had suffered a heart attack while jogging in a park near their home. Kyle had caught the first flight back to France. Fortunately, the attack had been a mild one. Although unexpected, Kyle had called him shortly after arriving at the hospital and had given him the good news. He'd, of course, told Kyle to take his time. Everyone knew their respective roles and jobs.

Kyle was very close to his parents as an only child. His parents were French, but Kyle's father loved all things British—especially the food. Garrett had joked that the heart attack resulted from Kyle's father's love of bangers and mash. Kyle had responded that it was more likely a result of his mother's *Mocha Pots de Créme*. They continued joking for a few more minutes about how a Frenchman could become so enamoured with British traditions. This led Kyle to reveal that his father named him after a former schoolmate and best friend who was British. At least before they hung up, Kyle had been laughing again.

Garrett checked his phone. He hadn't noticed it in the bazaar's craziness, but Kyle had left him a text message. Kyle had apparently caught an earlier flight and landed at Atatürk a half hour ago. He typed out a reply.

Come to my place. I have a surprise for you tonight.

His stop was coming up. Garrett stood and moved toward the doors. He'd transfer lines and take the next tram to Taksim Square then walk home from there. It was a nice day, anyway. He wove his way through the narrow streets of Cihangir, past all the antique shops and the café, where he frequently got his breakfast. When he turned the corner onto his street, he saw Kyle standing outside his building. Garrett smiled and lifted his hand in greeting.

"So, want to tell me about this surprise you have? Sounds... scintillating."

Garrett opened the door to the building, and they used the steps up to his flat, forgoing the lift. Within moments, they were inside. "I ran into Emir today at the bazaar. He suggested we should get out and experience the celebrations after sunset. He even volunteered to be our tour guide. So I thought if you were already here…"

Kyle relaxed on the settee. "Sounds like fun. The three of us. All… together."

Garrett turned his back and headed for the bar. He needed a drink. All the suggestions and innuendos flying around today were getting to him. If he wasn't careful, he'd end up taking Emir and Kyle up on their offers. And why was it that both men had propositioned him on the same day? Granted, there had been some heated looks between the three of them almost since the day they respectively met, but Garrett had made his position clear to both men.

He moved around the sofa so he could look at Kyle. "Did the two of you work this out together? It seems awfully convenient that both you and Emir say almost the same thing to me on the same day."

"No. But I'm not above taking advantage of a situation." Kyle stood and took a couple of steps closer to Garrett. "Apparently, our Turkish friend has the same style of thinking. I knew I liked him for good reason."

Kyle slid his hands over Garrett's shoulders. Not even the fires of hell could melt the ice, freezing his feet to the floor. His heart beat with the intensity of a timpani drum at presto tempo and his ears rang as if a bell cymbal had been struck right beside his ear. He shouldn't allow this, but Kyle's touch had made him a willing prisoner. Kyle leaned in and tilted his head. Their lips were only a few centimetres apart. After over a year of pent-up desire, Garrett was finally about to taste Kyle LaFleure. Garrett's hands shook as he placed them on Kyle's hips. His fingers dug in reflexively.

"*Non*. Not yet."

He stiffened—and not with desire—as Kyle backed away. "What?" he exclaimed as he backed away toward the kitchen.

"Don't worry, *mon cheri*. Before the sun rises, I have a feeling our lips will meet, but this is not the right time."

"And why should I play your bloody game? I could come over there right this second and take what I want."

Kyle nodded. "You could, but you know I'm right. There's some... *thing* missing. Some... thing necessary to make the moment perfect. If we hold off on our desires until the right time, then I promise it'll be an experience you'll never forget."

Garrett frowned. Now he understood Emir's disappointment earlier much better. Waiting was complete bollocks. He looked back at Kyle. The man shifted his stance and Garrett clearly saw the outline of an erection beneath Kyle's trousers. Well, at least he wasn't the only one suffering.

"Fine. So what do we do until this some... *thing* arrives?"

Kyle smiled. "What all good, civilised people do—Have a cup of tea."

"You hate tea." Garrett smirked.

"Fine, you have tea and I'll have an espresso," Kyle said, shrugging.

Chapter Four

G arrett, Kyle and Emir walked the streets of Sultanahmet in the Fatih district. It was almost a carnival-like atmosphere. The energy was so different from the daylight hours over the past four weeks. White lights strung across the street glowed in the darkness and music filled the air. Delicious scents enticed Garrett's stomach, resulting in a rumble. He'd heard there was a huge celebration at the end of the month, but he'd never imagined something on this scale. There was laughing and singing, the streets spilling over with people.

"You are enjoying the celebration?" Emir asked while looking over at Kyle and Garrett.

Garrett put his hand on Emir's arm, squeezing it gently. "Yes, thank you. This has been a night I will never forget. I know you haven't eaten yet. I made the three of us reservations at the Terrace Marmara Restaurant at the Blue House Hotel."

Kyle whistled. "Fancy."

He shrugged. "We're celebrating, right? Besides, after the construction begins in earnest next week, we'll all be too tired at night to do more than robotically feed ourselves, then collapse into bed."

"For the two of you, maybe, but I've been hard at work carving your columns and fountains for several months already. However, I make sure not to work beyond what's reasonable. It would be a shame to give up all the activities I enjoy—especially those that require great stamina. Now then, thank you for your consideration of making the reservations. A delicious meal is almost the perfect way to end the evening."

"Almost?" Kyle asked.

Emir smiled, "Well, the thing that would make it perfect is not something we are ready for yet." He looked at Garrett. "Soon, I hope."

The honey sound of Emir's accented voice washed over him, its promise blatant. Emir had been very careful about not touching either of them anytime they were in a public place, but Garrett's skin frequently burned from even the most casual touches when they were in private. Standing here in the middle of a crowded street, Garrett hoped his desires weren't as plain to see on his face as he feared they might be.

Garrett looked at Kyle and saw his smirk. Apparently, Garrett's acting skills weren't worthy of the West End. Kyle moved toward Emir and stood next to him. One pair of obsidian eyes and one pair of blue ones stared at him in expectation. All he had to do was concede, and the three of them would finally get to work burning off the caldera of lust that had been churning deep inside them, waiting for the perfect moment to erupt.

"If we don't hurry, we'll be late for our reservations."

It only took them a few minutes to walk to the hotel from the park. As they rode the lift to the rooftop restaurant and the host escorted to their table, Garrett felt Emir's and Kyle's focus on him, and the weight of their expectation hung heavy in the air.

The summer breeze blew gently as they sat at their table. The blue mosque showed in the darkness across the street. Its immense size completely obscured the horizon. The minarets speared the inky sky. A plate of appetisers rested on the table. Garrett particularly enjoyed the *paçanga*. He watched as Kyle sipped his wine and Emir drank his water.

"So, have we non-Muslims properly celebrated Ramadan?"

"In Turkey, we call it Ramazan, and yes, I believe you can now say you have celebrated our holiest of months."

Garrett sat back as the server placed a plate of Ottoman kebabs in front of him. Kyle hummed appreciatively at his chicken *cordon bleu*, and Emir quickly dug into his sultan kebabs. Of course, Garrett probably would be hungry as well after fasting all day. He knew Emir had eaten a light meal shortly after sunset, but for a man of his size, he needed fuel regularly.

I guess reflecting on your blessings and thinking of those less fortunate, like those who are starving, is part of the whole being an observant Muslim during Ramazan.

Garrett wasn't a religious man, but he could appreciate Emir's faith and beliefs. It was like how he felt when he'd first come out. His family had said repeatedly that they didn't understand it. What was it that made him the way he was? Garrett's response always had been, 'You don't have to understand it, but I ask that you respect it.' He looked at different religions the same way. Garrett smiled at Kyle and saluted Emir. Then he dug into his meal.

Garrett watched as the excavator dug out the land for the hotel's foundation. It was day one and things were officially underway. He saw Kyle standing off to the side, speaking with the general contractor. Hopefully, the workers would pour the footings and basement walls in the next week. Then it would be a long twenty-eight days before the real construction would begin.

They wouldn't utilise Emir's talents on site until there were actual walls, but as he'd said, he'd been hard at work since signing the contract. Emir had also said that he planned on creating cast mouldings that would surround every arched door in the building. The ending design of the hotel had drawn inspiration from the great mosques and historical buildings, such as the Hagia Sophia and Topkapı Palace. However, the guest suites would have all the modern conveniences such as Wi-Fi, Sub Zero outfitted mini kitchens, high-definition flat screens and multiple dual-line telephones. Not to mention, of course, the custom furnishings, top-of-the-line linens with genuine Turkish rugs and wall hangings, floor-to-ceiling windows that would take advantage of the views of the Bosphorus, marble bath suites with deep soaking tubs and personalised concierge service.

Garrett waved to Kyle, and he started walking his way. It had been a week since their adventure during the last night of Ramazan. Kyle's prediction hadn't come true that evening, as Garrett had managed to resist the two men's temptations. However, watching Kyle's sleek form stride across the construction site dissolved Garrett's resolve a fraction more. He'd been on hundreds of construction sites since he became a project manager. Never had the visage of a hard hat turned him on or a sturdy pair of work boots made him think of the owner's elegant feet walking around Garrett's flat barefoot.

"You needed something?"

"Yes..." Garrett cleared his throat and looked down at his tablet with the workflow schedule. "Um, so everything seems to be going smoothly. The soil isn't giving the excavator a hard time or anything?"

"No, once we get through the sixty to seventy meters of sediment, we'll reach the substrate, which, based on our survey, comprises a combination of chert, sandstone, claystone, greywacke, shale, and crystallised limestone. Assuming we don't hit any major limestone deposits, we should be able to lay the footings within a week."

That went along with the schedule, so Garrett was happy. His job as the project manager-superintendent was basically to run the three-ring circus. The general contractor and any independent foremen reported to him, and Garrett was the one who scheduled the work, ordered the supplies, and kept things running on time and on budget.

"Good. I was planning to check in with Emir this afternoon. Do you want to come and see what he's been working on?"

"Sure. I have to say that I'm most excited to see the *hamam* pieces. He said a couple of days ago that he's always wanted to work on a *hamam*. He's had some ideas for the mosaics, the fountain and the carved back décor for behind the *kurnas* floating around in his head for years. The drawings were amazing, but listening to him talk about the process the other day really got me excited."

"You saw him the other day?" Garrett hadn't seen the Turk since the night they'd all gone out.

Kyle nodded and looked over his shoulder as one of the crew gave a shout. "Yes, we met for supper, then he took me to see the palace. It has been very handy having a personal tour guide. He knows all the best local places and is so much more invested in telling the history of his city at the tourist stops."

Garrett wasn't sure how to feel about Kyle's revelation. He hadn't realised that Kyle and Emir were spending so much time together. On one hand, he was glad for the two men. Just because Garrett had rules for personal involvement and business didn't mean that Kyle and Emir needed to—or even should—restrict themselves. On the other hand, his insides churned with jealousy.

"Sounds as if you had a good time. I've been meaning to visit the palace, especially since several areas served as inspiration for the interior."

Kyle took a step closer to Garrett. "I'm sure he'd be happy to take you."

Garrett didn't want to impose on Kyle and Emir's time together. He gave a little smile. "We'll see."

Garrett knocked on one of the wide wooden doors to Emir's workshop. The artist used an old fire station as his base of operations. The doors were open to allow air to circulate, but he didn't see Emir anyplace, so Garrett walked in.

Inside were various works in progress and supplies. Piles of moldings and round arches, along with the decorative inserts that would anchor the moldings on the corners, lay curing on plastic sheeting. Emir had told him that it would make things vastly easier and more cost effective if he readied some of the masonry off-site then installed it once the building was ready.

Garrett walked toward one pile and studied it closer. "Amazing. How did he make it look so old?"

"It's a multi-step process."

Garrett spun around and nearly dropped his jaw at the sight of Emir standing in the summer sun with only a thin sweat-soaked T-shirt covering his broad chest. His gaze travelled down Emir's frame, lingering a fraction of a second more on the area of his hips, before following a pair of long legs encased in sturdy work trousers.

"Garrett?"

He jerked his head up and he looked right at Emir's lips. Big mistake.

Emir took several steps forward. "Are you all right? You seem disorientated and rather flushed. Were you out in the sun for long?"

Garrett spun and tried covertly to adjust himself, something he frequently found himself doing around both Kyle and Emir. As for the sun, it was beating down outside Emir's workshop. Since they'd crossed into July, it was now consistently hot, and Garrett was never without a bottle of water, hat and sunblock. He'd learned the hard way that dealing with sunburn while working on constructions sites was a miserable experience. Also, being dehydrated when working around heavy equipment was a safety hazard. Frankly, he valued his own life.

"I'm sorry. What were you saying when you walked in?"

Emir strolled over and stood next to Garrett, looking down at the mouldings. "Actually, I was answering your question. The way I age the stone is a multi-step process. First, I pour the concrete into the forms and let it dry. Then I strip the forms and pour an acid mixture of vinegar and lemon juice all over the surface. This opens up the pores, if you will. Then to achieve the patina of old stone, I rub it with manure and compost. For the exterior pieces, I'll wet it and dry it in both sun and shade repeatedly."

"Which ones are these?"

"These interior doors should not look weathered, but the design requires some aging to give the appearance that they were built during Ottoman times."

Garrett turned his head and studied the man next to him. "You really are a genius. I'm honored that you agreed to work with us on this project. I know you spend a lot of your time doing restorations and renovations, not new construction."

Emir faced Garrett. "Your proposal intrigued me. Also, the sound of your cultured British accent had my *çük* hard and my fingers flying on the keyboard of my laptop to find an image of you through your company website."

Garrett looked around the workshop, trying to focus on anything other than the heat in Emir's eyes. He saw a much larger casting on the other side of the room and started toward it. "What is...?"

He never made it more than a couple of feet. Emir gripped Garrett's hand and pulled him back. He wrapped his arm around Garrett's waist and slammed their lips together. At first, Garrett remained stiff, but within moments, his body capitulated to Emir's demands.

Emir slid his tongue between his lips and Garrett moaned as Emir's flavour mingled with his. Garrett wrapped his arms around Emir's neck and he pushed himself harder against the larger man. He was so warm, so masculine, so perfect. Emir gripped Garrett's ass, making him gasp and allowing Emir's tongue to possess him more thoroughly. Garrett almost fell backward, and he panicked until he realised he wasn't falling—Emir was guiding him. A warm, solid surface hit Garrett's back, and Emir insinuated a leg between his. Emir had a few inches in height on Garrett, so he lifted slightly to make their cocks rub together.

Emir released Garrett's lips and buried his nose in Garrett's neck. "Do not run from me again, *canım*."

"Well, this looks cosy!"

Garrett whipped his head toward the entrance and saw Kyle standing there with his arms crossed. He pushed Emir away and took several steps, only to be captured by Emir's powerful arm around his waist.

"I told you, *canım*, no more running."

He glanced back over his shoulder while he stiffened in fury. "Let me go, Emir." He turned to look at Kyle. "I'm sorry. I didn't mean for this to happen." He glanced back at Emir and scowled. "Actually, I didn't make this happen. I know the two of you have been..."

Kyle walked toward the pair of them—stalked them was a better description. Garrett squirmed a little but froze when the evidence of Emir's desire came into contact with his ass.

"We've been touring the city and sampling the local restaurants, trying to figure out the best way to seduce you. It looks like Emir finally got tired of all the subtle approaches. All I have to say is it's about time." He captured Garrett's face between his hands and kissed him—hard.

Oh, bloody fucking hell!

He ripped away from Kyle and stared into the man's blue eyes. "I shouldn't. God knows I... But pray he forgives me, because I must."

He grabbed Kyle's shoulders and dragged him in for another kiss. The two men he'd been dreaming about every night pinned him between them. Emir held Garrett's hips, while he licked tiny trails of fire along Garrett's neck. Kyle's mouth gave Garrett a new appreciation of the word seduction. It differed from Emir's conquering and explosive style, but heady all the same. Garrett was in absolute heaven. He had one hard cock pressing against his arse, and another rubbing against him through the lightweight summer trousers he'd taken to wearing while in Turkey.

Kyle pulled out of the kiss and smoothed a wayward strand of Garrett's hair. "I've wanted to do that for almost a year and a half."

While Garrett could admit to the same, there was a very genuine risk of excessive anticipation amplifying a genuine desire. He didn't know if he could stand to hear that Kyle had built up the experience so much in his mind that the reality was lacklustre. But at the same time, Garrett had to know, because his heart was pounding a thousand kilometres per second and he could have sworn there were heavenly choirs echoing through his head.

"Was it worth it?" Garrett asked softly.

Kyle studied Garrett for several heartbeats. His chest constricted before Kyle's blue eyes softened and he smiled.

"Better than I frequently dreamed."

Garrett let out a long breath. He leaned back against Emir. "So what now?"

Emir tightened his arms around Garrett's waist and he reached out with his other arm to bring Kyle in close. Garrett watched Emir and Kyle share a kiss. While Garrett didn't think of himself as submissive in any way, watching the two men kiss was like witnessing two alpha males converge for dominance. However, instead of one finally submitting, they found a middle ground, and it was the most erotic thing Garrett had ever witnessed.

Emir's dark hair and dusky complexion next to Kyle's blond and fair skin had Garrett hardening even further behind his zipper. Bloody hell, he'd give anything to watch those two men writhe naked on a bed. Almost as if it had a mind of its own, Garret's hand came up and he brushed his fingertips where their lips pressed together.

They broke the kiss, then Kyle turned to look at Garrett. "Are you okay, *mon cheri*?"

He nodded. Garrett looked at Emir and received a soft kiss on his fingertips. He didn't know what to do at this point. He'd never been in a situation like this before. Having crossed into his thirty-eighth year last November, Garrett was no novice at relationships. Some had lasted longer than others, but all followed the same pattern. He would meet a man, strike up conversation, determine if they were compatible, if there was mutual attraction, then they'd end up in bed and comfortably exist in each other's lives until the fire had burned its course. But whatever power was drawing him, Kyle and Emir together felt almost celestial, and Garrett certainly didn't have any experience with the metaphysical world. He was a simple guy from Bristol.

Emir adjusted them so Garrett now faced the Turk, and Kyle was at his back. This placement in the middle was seriously growing on him. There was definitely something to be said about being cocooned in two pairs of masculine arms, which was another unusual feeling for Garrett. In all his previous relationships, he'd assumed the more dominant or active role in sex, but right now, the thought of Emir or Kyle or even both men filling him was making Garret's head rush.

"I suggest we all enjoy a light supper, then have a little talk. I will tell both of you I'm not in this for a quick—what's the word?—fling?" Emir said.

Kyle tilted his head to the side of Garrett. "Have you done a three-some before?"

"No, but I don't sense a greater yearning for one of you over the other. So unless I'm misreading the situation, I'd like to explore the possibility of us as a unit. Have either of you done this before?"

He shook his head quickly, but he sensed a hesitation from Kyle behind him. Garrett turned to look at Kyle, who refused to meet his eyes. "Kyle?"

"Um... well, during my second year at university... But it was only one night."

His jaw dropped, and he heard Emir chuckle behind him. Suddenly, the mild-mannered Frenchman took on a whole new persona. "I didn't know you were such a kinky bastard!"

Kyle blushed, and Garrett laughed. It was fun to see the usually poised man flustered. "Well, at least one of us will know where all the parts go."

Both Kyle and Emir started laughing. Emir's deep voice resonated through the wide room while Kyle's had more of a musical quality. They complemented each other nicely.

Emir nipped at Garrett's neck, and Garrett trembled slightly.

"I think we are three intelligent enough men to figure that part out with little difficulty. It is when we are out of bed that will take a little bit more effort. But I am willing."

He received a kiss from Kyle then moaned as his soon-to-be lovers shared another kiss.

"Count me in," Kyle said.

Garrett was all for the sex, but he had concerns about the rest. How could three very different men, from three different countries, possibly make a harmonious relationship a reality? Granted, he and Kyle probably had a bit more in common, both being from Western Europe. Plus, Kyle had lived in London for five years, so they shared similar living arrangements, but his values and upbringing mirrored that of his countrymen. Then again, Istanbul was a modern urban city, even with its core of traditional values, so it wasn't as if Emir was unfamiliar with the world outside Turkey.

He looked at both Kyle and Emir, their expressions mimicking each other's—full of expectation, excitement and hope. Who was he to say the situation was impossible? For now, Garrett would agree, but it would be with some reservation. One of them had to keep a level head.

"Okay."

Chapter Five

Emir followed Kyle and Garrett into the apartment. He was still reeling from the reality of finally sharing the passion that had been building between the three of them for the past several months. In his workshop, he'd made sure that he appeared in control and confident, but deep inside, Emir knew there were many obstacles ahead of them if this relationship had any chance of growing.

He'd been inside Garrett's apartment on a few occasions, but never with the express purpose of making love. He watched Garrett immediately head straight for the bar and pour a drink. Clearly, the man was nervous. While Emir didn't drink alcohol, he could relate to the desire for some type of relaxant to deal with the anxiety of the situation. He looked over at Kyle to gage his reaction, but the man seemed completely calm and confident.

Well, that makes one of us.

Emir moved toward Kyle. He took the man's hand, then pulled him into a kiss. The kiss started out soft, Kyle's flavour rich and spicy. Emir put his hand on the back of Kyle's neck, gripping the end strands of

Kyle's hair and probing deeper with his tongue. Kyle wrapped his arms around Emir's waist and he let himself sink into the embrace. There was a weight on his shoulder and he recognised Garrett's aftershave drifting toward him from behind. The citrus scent reminded him of the sumac his *anne* used on her dumplings. Garrett's lips touched the back of Emir's neck and he instantly felt as though he was complete. He ground his renewed erection against Kyle's stomach and felt an answering press along his thigh.

There was a buzzing sound. At first, Emir thought it might result from the lack of oxygen flowing to his brain until Kyle backed away from their kiss with a smile.

"Is that a phone in your pocket or is there something you need to share with us?"

Emir frowned. He had a fairly good grasp of English, but he didn't understand Kyle. The buzzing sound started again and Emir felt vibrations in his pants. Oh! He shook his head and smiled at Kyle, then dug his phone out of his work pants. As he did, he couldn't believe that he'd been about to make love to these two men as filthy as he was. He'd have to ask Garrett if he could bathe before they went any further.

When he looked at the screen, he saw his *babba's* name and number. "Please, excuse me. It is my father."

Kyle moved away, and Emir stepped through the French windows and out onto the terrace. *"Alo, baba! Gün seni nasıl tedavi edilir?"* It was their traditional greeting to each other to ask how the day was treating them.

"Allah has blessed me this day. Meriç has finally come and sought my blessing for your sister's hand."

Emir smiled. His little sister, Kayra, had been dating Meriç for two years. They were young, vibrant, and just starting their careers. Kayra had recently finished her master's degree in forensic science, and

Meriç his degree in medicine. There had been countless family dinners over the past year, during which Emir's parents had lamented Meriç's delay in asking permission to marry his sister. It may be seen as an old-fashioned custom in most of the world, but Emir's family was very traditional. Well, his parents were in any case.

Kayra was only twenty-five. Still young in Emir's opinion, but he had to keep reminding himself that his parents grew up in a completely different generation. Theirs had even been an arranged marriage. When Emir's mother was barely eighteen, her father betrothed her to a man she had never met.

Emir had been born a very short ten months after the wedding. Kayra, on the other hand, hadn't arrived for another ten years. Emir knew that over the course of their marriage, his parents had grown to love each other, but he never got the impression that they were in love. More like wonderful friends.

"That's fantastic news. I will call her later and congratulate her. I'm sure *Anne* is already making plans."

There was a groan over the phone, and Emir could almost picture his father rolling his eyes. He knew his mother was going to drive Kayra crazy with all her opinions. Fortunately, Kayra was a strong woman, and Emir didn't think she'd allow their mother to completely take over.

"Emir, the engagement ceremony will take place on September twelfth and the marriage on October eighteenth. You, of course, will be there. Your mother said she will arrange for a proper guest to act as your companion."

Shocked into silence, Emir fumbled around for what his father had meant. Emir had never come out to his parents. He feared the two of them would have strokes if he told them he preferred a hard male body against his rather than a soft Turkish woman's. He'd avoided his mother's matchmaking skills for the past several years, but recently her efforts had been increasing and his father had even made several comments about finding a suitable woman for Emir to marry and get to work on starting a family.

By his parents' way of thinking, it was time for Emir to stop fooling around and settle down. He doubted, however, that they would ever be ready to meet Kyle and Garrett as Emir's intended partners.

"Of course I'll be there to celebrate my sister's marriage. Why would you think otherwise? However, why is the wedding so soon?"

He knew *in some things* his sister was traditional. Therefore, there was little chance of an impending addition to the family.

"Meriç has accepted a position in Adana. Kayra informed us she went behind our back and also accepted an offer for employment from their *polis*. I will see your sister properly married before I agree to let her accompany him."

Emir smiled. It was so like his little sister to do whatever she wanted, then inform their father. Then again, it was probably the only way she'd got so far in life as it was. Had it been up to their father, Kayra would still have a chaperone around the city everywhere she went. Emir knew his sister had been desperate to get out of their father's house for the past couple of years. Now it looked as though she was moving practically to the other side of the country. Adana was southeast of Istanbul on the Mediterranean side of the country. The area near the Syrian border was still recovering from a major earthquake and caught up in the refugee crisis. Emir had some feelings about his little sister moving to a region of unrest, but he also knew that was precisely why she and Meriç selected it.

He looked through the window and saw Garrett and Kyle kissing. Kyle had Garrett pinned against the sofa. There was a strip of pale skin visible on Garrett's back where Kyle had lifted his shirt. Kyle gripped

Garrett's ass, and Emir swore he almost felt the echo of the touch on his own flesh.

"You have been very busy these last months. No time for your family."

He let out a soft sigh and pinched the bridge of his nose. "My business takes a great deal of time. This new hotel is an extensive project. Also, how can you say I don't share time with the family? I share Al-Jumua with you every week."

"And how do you expect to meet a wife if you are working all the time?"

The window behind him allowed Emir to see that Kyle and Garrett had moved so that Garrett now had Kyle beneath him on the sofa. Emir moved his position on the terrace to get a better view. Both men had their shirts off and were grinding against each other as their lips met over and over. He couldn't believe he was missing this!

"*Baba*, I have to get back to work. I'll talk to you later."

"Emir Şahin, I'm speaking to you. You do not dismiss me. This is important. I'm talking about your future. Our family's future. You have an obligation—"

"To respect you, but not to obey. I have my life and live it as I see fit. As I said, I will speak with you later."

He hung up the phone. When his father got angry, there really was no negotiating with him. His father's name, Hakan, meant emperor. In Emir's experience, his father could be as autocratic as one, too. He walked inside the apartment, then put his phone down. He frowned when he saw that Garrett and Kyle had stopped what they were doing. Garrett stood and stepped in front of Emir.

"Is everything okay? I don't speak much Turkish, but things sounded a little heated out there."

Emir reached out and ran his hand down Garrett's chest. Garrett put his hand on top of Emir's and held it in place. He looked up and saw the concern in Garrett's eyes. He leaned in and kissed Garrett softly.

"Nothing to worry about, but thank you for caring. What I watched in here had my blood pressure rising higher than anything my father said. The two of you together are stunning."

Garrett kept his hand over Emir's and slid it across Emir's chest, over his nipples, then down his torso. Garrett's soft skin felt like silk beneath his work-roughened hands. He would have been worried about his coarse skin, but the look of complete rapture on Garrett's face had Emir pressing a little harder.

Garrett only had a thin trail of hair leading beneath the waistband of his slacks. Emir, in general, appreciated smooth skin on a lover. He didn't mind a little hair, but he'd never been attracted to a man with a full chest of fur. Emir looked down to see Garrett's erection tenting his trousers. It appeared of good size, and Emir wanted to feel it filling his mouth and throat.

Kyle stood from the sofa then walked behind Emir. He craned his head to follow him, but Garrett guided Emir's face around and captured his lips. Emir moaned. Kyle slipped his hands beneath the edge of his shirt, and Emir suddenly remembered his filthy state. He reluctantly reversed out of Garrett's kiss.

"I'm a mess. Before we go further, I'd like to bathe. Can I use your shower?"

Garrett looked over Emir's shoulder at Kyle, and the two shared a smile. The promise in Garrett's expression had Emir's body tightening more.

"You may. Only if we can watch." Garrett closed the distance between them and put his lips against Emir's ear. He whispered, "I want to see the water run off every curve and angle of your body. I want to see you stroke your cock as Kyle and I watch."

Emir swallowed hard. He stepped out from between the two men and walked down the hall toward the bathroom. He'd used the facilities before, so he knew where to go. Emir stripped his shirt over his head as soon as he entered the room. He quickly opened his pants. Emir adjusted the dial to set the temperature and selected the overhead water source, not the hand-held sprayer. He leaned against the back wall and removed his work boots. Kyle and Garrett came into the room. Garrett activated the ceiling heat lamps and radiant flooring as Emir stripped off his pants. The water cascaded over his face and head as he tilted it back.

It was so refreshing after the hot day. He washed his hair, then scrubbed the dirt and dust of his work away. As he rinsed, he heard mutterings. He looked up and saw Kyle and Garrett gawking at him. He'd forgotten that he was supposed to put on a show.

"Merde! Un homme ne doit pas être que magnifique."

Emir looked across the room. His rudimentary French was good enough that he could understand the basics of Kyle's whispered compliments. Emir tightened the muscles of his torso and spread his legs slightly so his men could get a good look at *everything*. His cock had softened, but under his soon-to-be lovers' appreciative looks, it filled once again.

Emir gripped his cock and gave it a few strokes. His ego rose a couple of notches at the identical, admiring expressions of Kyle and Garrett as it thickened and grew. Both men's eyes followed Emir's hand, and Kyle licked his lips.

His men were also naked, and Emir was just as happy to study their physiques. Garrett was the oldest of the three of them, and his slightly seasoned body was delicious, in Emir's opinion. Garrett's hair was mostly light brown, but there was a subtle mixture of grey strands threading through the short waves. His green eyes had an inner glow that rivalled the richest sultan's treasures. His body was still trim and firm, even if it didn't have the freshness of youth. The light dusting of hair that began between Garrett's dusky nipples was almost shadow-like until it coalesced in a trim thatch that surrounded his cock. Garrett's cock was long with just the right amount of width. It currently stood tall against his stomach.

Kyle was very fair with blond hair and bright blue eyes. The soft, medium-length strands were just long enough for Emir to grab when he wanted to hold Kyle prisoner to his kiss, and those blue eyes reminded Emir of the lights that lit up the city every night. Kyle was thinner than Garrett, but seemed to hold an inner strength that belied his smaller frame. Emir had felt Kyle's large hands on his body—hands that gripped Emir's body earlier with a fierce determination. The two men were delicious treats awaiting his sampling on a banquet table, and Emir felt himself being drawn toward them, eager for their sweetness.

Just as he crossed the room, the two of them moved. The three of them met in the middle of the room. Emir kissed Garrett first, then Kyle. He lost focus on whose hand touched which man's body part, but it didn't matter. All that did matter were the blissful sensations of male hands on him for the first time in months. Until he'd kissed Garrett earlier, Emir hadn't realised how starved he'd become for another's touch.

Despite the warm, humid air of the bath, Emir's skin quickly chilled without the hot water cascading over him. He tugged and lured Garrett and Kyle under the spray with him. The shower design of the apartment was perfect for them. Emir couldn't imagine enjoying an experience like this in his small apartment on the second level of his workshop.

Kyle dipped his head and sucked on Emir's nipple right as Garrett wrapped a firm hand around his cock.

"Evet," Emir said, as he sucked in a breath.

"You like that?" Kyle asked.

He nodded and gripped Kyle's shoulder hard while locking his knees so he wouldn't collapse from the pleasure coursing through him. Garrett moved and the heat of his lover's body warmed him from behind, placing him in the middle. Gripping Emir's hips, Garrett pulled him back. Garrett slid his cock between Emir's cheeks, and Emir tightened in anticipation. He couldn't remember the last time a man filled him.

Totally focused on the gentle gyrations of Garrett's hips, Emir let out a shout when wet heat engulfed his cock. His eyes flew open, and he looked down to see Kyle kneeling before him. The man's damp blond hair brushing against his flesh cooled the heat generated by Emir's arousal. He cradled Kyle's head, and Emir's mind short-circuited with the incredible suction of Kyle's mouth. He knew he was thicker than many men, so the Frenchman's ability to take all of him was impressive—a talent Emir was truly thankful for.

Garrett spread Emir's ass cheeks and began to grind in earnest. Emir's head was guided around by Garrett who took a kiss from him. Their mouths came together, their tongues moving slowly, almost in identical rhythms as Garrett's cock. Emir moaned, but he did nothing to interrupt his lovers' rhythms. Involuntary contractions of his muscles made his body flex and tremble. Sounds of delight and hunger from all three men filled the steamy air.

Emir tilted his head back against Garrett's shoulder. The Brit was slightly shorter than he was, so it naturally made Emir's back arch and his hips tilt toward Kyle's ministrations. Garrett twisted and pinched Emir's nipples. Emir spread his legs wider when Kyle tapped his inner thigh. His reward was a slick finger circling the tight ring of muscle guarding his hole. He hissed and bore down, eager once again to have something inside him. He tried to take an inventory of body parts, but his brain was so flooded with endorphins that simple arithmetic was beyond him.

One of Kyle's fingers breached his body while his throat clenched around the head of Emir's cock. Licks of fire spread up from his chest and down to his groin where his nipples burned from being pinched, tugged and rolled. There was an intense moment of pressure, then another finger entered him. The angle was perfect to rub over his prostate, and Emir's orgasm threatened.

"Oh, no you don't. Not yet. Not till we get Garrett inside you."

Kyle's voice was slightly hoarse from having Emir's cock deep, possessing its tight channel. But the growly quality was the most arousing Emir had ever heard.

"Please. Now. Yes."

Garrett chuckled behind him. "Incomplete sentences... That means we're doing something right."

He opened his eyes to meet Garrett's green gaze. "How's this for a sentence—I'll bend over that gigantic bed in the other room and have you fuck me, while I swallow Kyle's cock whole."

"*Oui!*" Kyle jumped up then turned off the water.

The bath became suddenly silent except for the sounds of their heavy breathing. Garrett gathered towels for each of them off the warming rack. The three of them trod through the alcove that served as Garrett's study and into the bedroom. Kyle tossed the towel and crawled onto the platform bed. The top of the mattress only reached Emir's knees. This would make fucking from the side more difficult, but he was confident that between three intelligent men, they could be creative and figure out a way.

Slowly stroking his cock, Kyle asked, "Where's your stuff?"

Garrett walked down the side of the bed to the attached nightstand. Beneath it sat a wicker basket. When Garrett bent over, his gorgeous ass was on full display. Emir even got a peek of the little pink ring hidden in the furrow between Garrett's cheeks. When Garrett stood, disappointment filled Emir until he saw the lube and condom in Garrett's grasp.

"You'd better get more than one, *mon cheri*."

"But I thought..."

Kyle knee-walked across the bed until he was in front of Garrett. He wrapped his arms around Garrett's waist and kissed him in the middle of his chest. "You think any of us are going to be satisfied with just one round?"

Garrett reached for the basket and dumped the remaining condoms on the mattress. Emir's laughter mixed with Kyle's. It was nice to experience a little fun with his sex. While he'd been afraid that adding a third person into the bedroom would make for an awkward dynamic, in reality—or at least *their* reality—the balance felt right. Not to say that he didn't plan on having quality one-on-one time in the near future, but for this first time together, it made Emir feel as though they were all starting out on equal footing.

The two men tumbled back onto the mattress after Kyle tugged on Garrett's arm. Emir didn't want to wait around to join in on the fun, so he positioned himself on the bed next to Kyle and Garrett, observing their heated embrace. He slid his hand down Garrett's back. When he got to Garrett's ass, Emir gave it a squeeze, then nipped the round flesh. The muscles beneath his lips clenched. Kyle spread his legs farther and Garrett slid into the opening. Emir heard Kyle gasp, and he looked up to see Garrett sucking on the Frenchman's neck. Garrett and Kyle both ground their hips together, their hard cocks trapped between them. The air of the bedroom filled with the scent of their arousal and the warmth of the sun shining through the large floor-to-ceiling windows. At least Garrett kept the blinds lowered to prevent the outside world from entering their bedroom.

Emir adjusted his position, so he knelt behind Garrett, also between Kyle's legs. He separated Garrett's cheeks and licked. A popping sound followed as Garrett disengaged from Kyle's flesh with a cry. Emir licked across Garrett's hole again, the smoky flavour of Garrett's skin ambrosia to his long denied taste buds.

He stiffened his tongue and pushed against the tightly sealed opening. He swirled it around and around. Gradually, Garrett's flesh softened and Emir could get the tip of his tongue inside his lover's channel.

"*Foutre,* Emir, you should see his face. You are driving him wild. I've never seen eyes so bright. Don't stop. *Mon Dieu*, Garrett. *Oui!* There!"

Kyle's words fuelled Emir's efforts until he had to hold Garrett's hips to keep the man from humping Kyle as Garrett's need for stimulation increased. Emir's cock throbbed, and he knew if he didn't come soon, the agony of anticipation would go from sweet to painful. He picked up the bottle of lube and squeezed some onto his fingers. He slid them along Garrett's crease, rubbing over the hole Emir had opened with his tongue.

Garrett's head popped up. "Wait, I thought... who's fucking who?"

He leaned over and placed his lips against Garrett's ear, bracing his weight on his hands on either side of Kyle. "I'm going to fuck you, and you're going to fuck Kyle."

A soft whimper from beneath Garrett made Emir smile. Kyle lifted his knees until they rubbed the backside of Emir's arms. He gave Kyle's legs a caress as he moved back to his position behind Garrett. He couldn't really reach much of his other lover, since Garrett had Kyle pinned, but the two of them seemed to be getting along just fine. Emir pressed the tip of one finger inside Garrett. The man's tight clench indicated it had been some time since he'd had anything inside him. He pushed his finger deeper and heard dual moans from the top of the bed.

Garrett pressed back against Emir and he knew his man was ready for more. One finger became two. Garrett growled as Emir stretched his channel, rubbing over Garrett's gland.

"Easy, *mon cheri*. We need to make sure you're nice and open for him. You saw that monster between his legs. It was so heavy it couldn't even stand up straight," Kyle said while rubbing Garrett's back. "Now me, I have an entire collection of toys I've been shoving up my ass while fantasising about the two of you. Just give me a little slick and we'll get this beautiful cock where it belongs."

Allah, for a man who made his living drawing complicated works of art, Kyle's words had Emir thinking masterpiece. Emir reached between Garrett's legs and rolled a condom down his length. The man's flesh was tight and slick with evidence of his arousal. As per Kyle's instructions, he applied some lube to Kyle's hole, but gave the opening a quick check for compliance. He didn't want anyone getting hurt in their eagerness. Emir squeezed a generous amount of lube out on his hand, then wrapped it around Garrett's cock, coating it in the cool gel.

"Bugger and blast!" Garrett gave a couple of quick hard thrusts in Emir's grip, then looked down at Kyle, his breathing heavy. "How?"

"Like this. Want to see you."

Kyle gripped under his knees and held his legs up. Garrett placed his cock at Kyle's opening. He pushed in, slightly. Kyle tossed his head about on the pillow as he moaned. Emir stroked his cock as he watched Garrett fill Kyle inch by inch. In a little farther each time, then back out. Emir's own ass tingled with the desire to feel Garrett's rod against him again. When Garrett finally seated himself all the way inside Kyle, Emir took no time before he pushed three fingers deep into Garrett.

Garrett cried out and his body tightened around Emir's digits.

"Bloody fucking hell. I've never had it both ways. I'm going to come! You'd better get inside me, Emir, if we're all going to do this together."

He gave Garrett's balls a squeeze to hold off the man's release. Emir donned a condom and efficiently used the lube over the latex. He placed the tip of his cock against Garrett's opening and pressed his way inside. The intense heat and constriction of his lover's body had Emir frozen in place with only partial entry. As Garrett had done with Kyle, Emir used an advance-and-retreat method until he buried his entire length. He kissed the taut curve of Garrett's spine. Emir's body protested against the delay, but until he got some sign from Garrett, there was no way he would move.

"He's in, *mon cheri*. All the way, deep inside you. Can you feel his flesh throbbing with the need to claim you, as I do yours? We're all connected now."

Kyle's accent had thickened, and his voice had deepened. Emir continued to kiss Garrett's back and smooth his hands over every inch of Garrett's and Kyle's bodies that he could reach. Garrett moved his hips in small increments and Emir almost shouted in relief. They tried to find the right rhythm. Emir let Garrett set the initial pace. Being in the middle, the man could fuck Kyle in the way he wanted, and take Emir into his body at the speed and depth most comfortable.

Garrett's ass hugging him like a glove was an amazing experience, but soon Emir's body craved to take over. He slowly started driving his hips toward Garrett. Thrust by thrust, his speed increased until he was slamming into Garrett, which forced Garrett into Kyle at a rhythm that had the Frenchman begging for more. Emir gripped Garrett's hips tighter and adjusted the angle of his entry so that he was driving downward.

"Ah, God!" Garrett cried out.

The shout vibrated Emir's core. Harder and faster, Emir thrust. Sweat dripped down his forehead. The sounds of slapping, damp flesh filled the room. Emir looked down and watched his dark cock fill Garrett's stretched pink hole. Emir's orgasm came over him suddenly. Everything inside him sizzled, his fingertips tingled, the hair on the back of his neck stood, and his body convulsed as he shot into the latex.

Seconds later, Garrett's channel quivered as he came. Emir encircled Garrett's waist with one arm. With his other hand, he gripped Kyle's cock caught between their bodies. Pre-cum coated the hard flesh. Kyle secured his long legs around both Garrett and Emir. He dug his heels into Emir's back. Emir gave it only a couple of strokes before thick heat flooded his hand. Kyle's shout became muffled as he pressed his face against Garrett's neck.

The three of them unpiled. Emir's muscles quivered with exertion. Emir slid the condom off his cock. As he was about to sit up and try to locate a rubbish bin, one appeared over his head out of nowhere. He tossed the latex and then curled around Kyle. He put his arm over Kyle's waist and placed soft kisses along Kyle's shoulder. The man's sweaty chest heaved with laboured breaths. Beneath Emir's hand, Kyle's heart pounded.

"Are you okay?" he asked softly.

Kyle turned his head to look at Emir. "Are you kidding? I'm fantastic."

Kyle's blue eyes had a soft hazy glow to them and his lopsided smile tugged at Emir's heartstrings. Emir cupped Kyle's cheek and kissed him softly. Their tongues slowly rubbed against each other. Kyle rolled on top of Emir. The two of them shared lazy post-sex kisses and touches. Emir enjoyed Kyle's warm flesh over him. Kyle pulled out of their kisses and settled back on the mattress. Emir saw Garrett settle against Kyle's back. Garrett rested his hand on Emir's hip. His mind drifted in the lassitude only possible with complete peace. Maybe after a brief nap, he would make Garrett and Kyle some supper. It would be nice to sit on Garrett's terrace and watch the lights come to life along the Bosphorus.

Chapter Six

After almost two years of work, Kyle could finally see the physical evidence of his conceptualised design. With the revised plans, he'd drawn inspiration from the era of Classical Ottoman architecture. The lobby, *hamam*, and restaurant all featured domed ceilings. They planned to incorporate carved limestone pillars for non-structural detail throughout the interior. All the doorways would feature arched openings with detailed mouldings, and the hallways would have curved mosaic ceilings like those in the grand bazaar.

Some suites would have grotto-like soaking pools and steam rooms. The rooms in the hotel had a variety of shapes. Some were long, others octagonal or shaped like a star. In the centre of the structure was a gardened courtyard, where guests could take tea and relax near a fountain that Emir had designed. Kyle made a concentrated effort not to have one boxy space after another, as were most hotels. Where it wasn't possible to achieve the look he wanted structurally, he'd designed non-structural elements to give the room an appearance of the look he desired. For example, in the restaurant, he used false walls to create the rounded room beneath the dome that had the bonus of hiding access areas to the kitchen.

At this point in the construction process, all the framing and exterior walls were in place. At this point in the construction process, the workers had finished all the windows and exterior doors. Additionally, they had designed star-shaped cutouts into the dome of the hamam's hot room ceiling to allow rays of natural light. Kyle thought the stained-glass choices the interior designer had made for the lobby were perfect. They really added to the overall aesthetic the owners were trying to achieve. And the huge, carved, wooden front doors gave the hotel a fortress-like appearance. Fortunately, electronic openers aided the massive doors so guests wouldn't have to use the large metal rings to pull them open on their own.

Currently, there were multiple contractors working. One crew was laying the copper flashing on the three domes, while another was bricking the exterior. The crew would shingle the remaining part of the roof in synthetic slate. Inside, the plumbing was being roughed in. Then the electrical crew would come. Both processes would take some time. While the design of the building was intended to appear old, the functionality was fully modern and even forward-thinking in many areas.

"So, what do you think?"

Kyle looked over at Garrett. Every time he saw Garrett in a hard hat, he smiled, because the brim of the hat always had a tendency to slip down over Garrett's eyes. He was constantly fighting the thing.

"It looks great. The antique brick was a good choice. It adds character and looks perfect with the aged stone process Emir used on the quoins."

"I agree. As well, with all the construction taking place in the city, reclaimed brick is readily available. Emir was the one who gave me the contact for the wholesaler."

"Speaking of our lover, have you spoken with him? We didn't stay together last night, and when I tried calling him this morning, his phone just went to voicemail."

Garrett shook his head. "I got the same thing. He's seemed a little preoccupied over the last couple of days, but I know he's been working on carving the courtyard fountain. I'm sure he'll call when he surfaces from the limestone dust."

Kyle hummed. "I know it's only been a couple of months, but we've yet to go more than twelve hours without talking to one another. Last night when I asked him about coming over, he gave me this really *couillonnade* excuse."

"That's rather harsh, Kyle. Why are you so upset about this? We've spent nights apart."

Kyle turned to look back at the copper gleaming under the early fall sun. "You're right. It's this whole situation with his—Wait, what day is it today?"

"It's the eightee—Oh, bollocks! His sister's wedding is today. No wonder he's not answering his phone and has been so distracted."

When Emir had shared the news of his sister's engagement, the man had been very excited. However, when Kyle had asked him if he wanted them to accompany him to the event, Emir had frowned and told him that his family would never allow it. Only immediate family was going to be allowed at the ceremony. Kyle was disappointed, but he understood.

He'd been all set to let the situation go when Emir had revealed there would be a large wedding party for extended family and friends later this evening. Kyle had asked Emir what kind of gift he should give the couple. But Emir had once again informed him that such a thing would be inappropriate. At first, Kyle had thought it was because he wasn't Muslim, and both Kyle and Garrett had learned over the last couple of months how traditional Emir's parents were. However, Kyle had done some reading about Turkish weddings online and learned that while it was true that in some families only immediate relatives attended the ceremony, it seemed to be the trend that everyone and their cousin, and neighbour, went to the wedding party.

In more rural areas, some parties would last for days, with the entire village and anyone visiting, taking part. Kyle had then gone to Garrett with his information to get their lover's input. Garrett had been the one to tell Kyle that Emir wasn't out to his family, and that was probably his reasoning for the evasiveness, which only steamed Kyle further. Shouldn't that be something Emir would tell him? Then again, why hadn't Kyle taken the time to ask? Emir was so open with affection and his words when they were together in their flats that Kyle simply hadn't considered that possibility.

Kyle and Garrett walked toward the building. "I still think we should have least got Kayra a gift, even if Emir doesn't want us there. Emir's parents may have a rather antiquated view of the world, but Kayra doesn't. At least, not based on what Emir has told us about her. She'd probably appreciate the thought."

Kyle knew he was on the verge of pouting, but he couldn't seem to stop himself. It was as if now that he'd started talking, he couldn't stop venting his frustrations. It wasn't fair to Garrett. He wasn't the one Kyle was upset with.

Garrett stopped and turned, putting his hand on Kyle's shoulder. "I know you're hurt that Emir doesn't want us at the party, but are you really upset about the party or is there something else bothering you?"

Kyle knew he was probably blowing the whole situation out of proportion, but he really cared for Emir. In fact, if he were honest with himself, over the past six months since he'd arrived in Istanbul and had met Emir, Kyle had probably fallen in love with the Turk. Something special happened to him when he was with Emir. Kyle felt as though it was okay for him to relinquish the role of caregiver in the relationship. He'd always been a take-charge kind of guy. The one to make the plans, initiate discussions, the one who burnt dinner regularly.

While he didn't feel as though he was morphing his personality in Emir's presence, something mentally urged Kyle to accept his lover's help. For the first time, he felt as though it was okay to sit on the sofa and rest his head in Emir's lap, walk through the door of his or Garrett's apartment and ask for a hug after a hard day. Kyle had bottomed more in bed since the three of them got together than he probably had in the past ten years, and he loved it.

With the non-invite to his sister's big day, Kyle suddenly felt as though maybe he didn't mean as much to Emir as Emir meant to him. Emir may not be out to his family, even so, what was the harm in inviting close co-workers to an enormous party?

"I know he's not out, but it's not as if I expect him to lead me onto the dance floor and pull me into his arms. I just thought it would be nice for him to acknowledge us as a part of his life, even if we kept the true meaning on the down low."

"Remember, things are very different here. It's not like London or Paris, where individuals can be open and it's generally not thought of as catastrophic. While the gay population is slowly revealing them-selves here in Istanbul, Turkey is still a very conservative country. And from what I've gathered from Emir, his family is even more so. Emir has spent his whole life looking up to his father, doing everything to gain the man's respect. And let's face it, while we may keep our hands to ourselves in public, our eyes have a tendency to speak volumes when we are together—at least yours do. I love looking over at you and seeing those baby blues burn like the brightest flame. You, love, wear your heart in your eyes. Which is wonderful when we're all together, but I imagine terrifying when surrounded by unsuspecting family members." Garrett took a quick look around, then gave Kyle a one-arm hug. "He knows we're here for him."

Kyle leaned into Garrett's embrace for a moment. Garrett tended to be the voice of reason among the three of them. It was a good thing because Kyle knew he could get a little emotionally erratic. But he was French!

Garrett looked back down at his tablet with the day's work and order schedule in his grip. Kyle felt as if Garrett should have the thing welded to his body. Sometimes he had the urge to rip it from Garrett's hand and toss it in the Sea of Marmara. He took a deep breath and let it out. Getting upset and taking his frustration out on an innocent piece of electronics would not improve the situation.

Kyle saw the foreman of the plumbing crew waving him down. He gave Garrett's shoulder a pat before walking toward the main entrance. Kyle mentally prepared himself to talk to the man. The foreman didn't speak any French and spoke only a little English, but the two of them used Google Translate for a lot of their conversations. Kyle already had his tablet out and the app ready.

"Problem, Mr. Kyle."

"Yes?"

"*Hamam* plans say cool water in the dressing room will fall from four meter, but..." He made a bunch of gestures. "*Tesisat.* Ah..."

Kyle could see the foreman was uncertain how to explain the problem. He turned his tablet around and the foreman nodded, then quickly typed in what he wanted to say. He hit the final button, then showed Kyle the screen. Kyle read that the man claimed that once installed, the bells would be less than one meter above the guests' heads. Impossible! The plans state that the trio of rainfall showerheads should be mounted inside copper bells that are less than a meter in height. The bells were supposed to mount at the apex of the arched ceiling, which was four and a half meters tall. They'd gone with this design instead of one of Emir's custom fountains because the design team thought it added a uniqueness to the space. The design team decided to install private dressing cubicles around the edge of the room and incorporated continuous soft music to welcome guests as they checked in for their hamam experience.

"*Merde!*" He looked at the foreman, frowning. "Show me."

Kyle followed him through the main doors. Since he had never designed a *hamam* before, he'd consulted a company that designed and installed *hamams* for modern spas. Together, they'd gone through a design development phase that reflected the old world authenticity of the hotel, while using modern materials. After Garrett's plumbing crew finished with the boilers, radiant heat system, and pipes for the faucets, the company would assist Emir with the installation of the marble tiles, *kurna*, back panel decor, *cini* tiles, and mosaics. Also, the HVAC team needed to install the ventilation and air return system.

Kyle stepped into the area that would eventually become the lobby, freezing as the presence of the first dome hit him. It wasn't the first time he'd stood inside the structure, and it certainly wouldn't be the last. The dome wasn't on the same massive scale as the great mosques, but Kyle still felt its significance over his head. As much as he dreamed they had resources and time to dress out the interior of the domes with mosaics like the real mosques and palaces of the city, the reality was that this was a commercial property that needed to turn a profit in order to remain open. Plus, that would require them to hire another skilled artisan. Instead, they would use stencils and air guns to paint the domes of the lobby and the restaurant with Turkish art patterns.

Kyle saw the foreman standing at the entrance to the hall that led to the *hamam*. He hurried across the lobby to join the man and get to work, solving the disaster for the day.

Garrett watched Kyle walk inside with the plumber. Hopefully, there wasn't a major problem that would cause a delay in construction. Even though his company had said to spare no expense, it didn't mean that Garrett had a blank cheque to work with. He was still responsible for keeping the project on budget. He'd have to check in with Kyle later to find out why the gaffer's expression was so tense.

The other issue for the day, of course, was their missing third. Now that the hotel's main structure was up and the interior infrastructure was being installed, Emir worked on site more than he had over the summer, which worked out brilliantly for Garrett and Kyle because they had multiple chances to ogle Emir as he manoeuvred and installed heavy stone. The other side to that coin was that watching the action could frustrate as well. Since it put all of Emir's assets on display, it made Garrett want to grab his lover and pin him to a wall. Not really an option at a busy construction site.

He understood Kyle's disappointment about not being invited to Kayra's wedding. However, unlike Kyle, Garrett understood Emir's position with more empathy. He had absolutely no intention of forcing Emir out of the closet. Not that he thought Kyle was trying to push Emir out into the open, but Garrett knew that keeping their relationship underground had been hardest on Kyle. And while Garrett felt a certain amount of exclusion, he supposed it was simply part of dating someone in the closet. He'd been there before, and it had never really bothered him. Of course, that might have been because Garrett was a private person, anyway. He'd never made a habit of broadcasting his preferences or relationships. Not that he'd didn't enjoy a night out with a lover, but Garrett preferred to keep things casual and low key while in public.

To Garrett's way of thinking, he and Kyle were lucky to have Emir in their lives at all. Usually, for at least half the week, the three of them were at either Kyle's or Garrett's flat eating, relaxing and making love before curling around each other until dawn. Garrett had even got used to Emir crawling out of bed for Fajr, the pre-dawn prayer. The call to worship throughout the city would echo through the windows of the flat.

He'd been in his share of relationships over the years, but this partnership between him, Kyle, and Emir was so far working out better than anything he'd experienced in the past. He'd come to really care for both men. Garrett wouldn't say that he was in love, not yet, but the potential was definitely there.

Garrett reviewed his list. He needed to contact the electrical supplier and make sure that they were still on schedule for the delivery next week. Garrett had placed the order a month ago for all of the controls, breakers, boxes, conduit, fittings, wire and consoles as outlined by the electrical engineers from Kyle's firm. The hotel system would be state of the art to coincide with their anticipated five-star rating. That meant that each guest suite would have multi-zone touch panel lighting and temperature controls, smart televisions, multiple phone and fibre ethernet outlets, as well as everything necessary for in room wireless connectivity. That didn't include any of the specialised lighting controls necessary in the restaurant, or everything necessary for the public areas. Personally, Garrett was very glad he didn't have to worry about actually installing any of the snaking mess.

He checked his phone for any messages. There was only one from Edward—Garrett's mentor and the officer of the company who was directly overseeing the project. The man was most likely checking in on the progress. Garrett sent weekly update reports back to London, but he sometimes still got calls. Garrett considered waiting until the end of the day, but he knew that Edward's calls were usually important and not just meant to bother him. Most of the time it was because the CEO had been on Edward's back, asking for progress from Garrett's perspective on the ground, not just a typed status report of the systems being installed.

He clicked open his contacts and was about to connect when the roofers started driving nails into the copper flashing. He eyed the on-site trailer that served as a mobile office—probably a better idea. As he walked across the ground, dust flew up into the air. It had been a very dry summer, and while that worked in their favour for staying on schedule, it sometimes made breathing difficult in the city. He pulled open the door. The hot air hit him like a wall, since there was no air conditioning in the trailer.

He pulled at the collar of his shirt. Garrett remembered on his first job that he'd been convinced he needed to maintain an air of authority so he'd always worn suits. However, his dry cleaning bill had quickly taught him the error of his ways. Now Garrett always traveled with suits in case he was required to meet with contractors in an office setting, but on days when he was on site, he dressed in sturdy work trousers, utility shirts and heavy boots.

Garrett sat and put his feet up on the desk. He tapped the icon for Edward's contact number. As he listened to the rings chiming over and over, he studied the blueprints spread out on the drafting table next to the desk. He practically had the things memorised, but there was something about the blue sheets with white intersecting lines and notations that always drew his attention, even for the millionth time.

"Hello?"

"You rang?"

"I did. How are things going?"

If this was the only reason for the call, Garrett was going to have a little bit of fun.

"It's completely gone balls-up. The plumbers don't know their arses from their tits and half the bricks are dust."

There was nothing but silence coming through the phone. Garrett smiled.

"Are you taking the piss?"

"Maybe."

"You tosser."

Garrett laughed loudly. It was a fortunate thing his boss had become a close friend in the fifteen years Garrett had worked for the company. He'd started right out of university, and Edward had taken Garrett under his wing. The door to the trailer opened and Kyle walked in. He arched an eyebrow and Garrett lifted his arm. Kyle walked over and snuggled against Garrett.

He lifted his chin, silently asking for a kiss. He listened with half an ear as Edward went on and on about the stuff Garrett already had under control. Kyle bent down and once their lips touched, the half ear Garrett was listening with faded out. Kyle backed out of the kiss. He knocked Garrett's legs off the desk, then straddled Garrett's lap.

Garrett adjusted Kyle's position until their bodies snuggled together. He grasped Kyle on the back of his neck, then pulled the man in for another kiss. Their tongues slowly rubbed against each other. Kyle smoothed his hands up and down Garrett's chest. He used his nimble fingers to unfasten the first couple of buttons on Garrett's shirt. Garrett shifted, trying to give his cock more room inside his jeans.

"*Oi*! Do you think you could stop snogging LaFleure long enough to have a conversation with the man who signs your paychecks?"

He gave Kyle's ass a grope, then a pat. "Oh, sod off," he said into the phone. "How do you know LaFleure is even here, let alone assume we're macking on company time?"

Edward scoffed. "I feared for the safety of my boardroom several times because of all the sparks between you two. As well, I bet Hugh a score that within two weeks of your landing, the two of you would shag like bunnies. So I'm hoping you're going to confess all, and I can go collect my winnings."

He looked at Kyle who shrugged. Clearly, it was up to him whether they revealed their relationship. But what about Emir? Garrett certainly wasn't going to out their other lover. So it was confess to part or continue to hide all.

"Say no more."

Garrett rolled his eyes. "I haven't said *anything*."

"And that tells me everything I need to know. Listen, I didn't really call to have a good old chinwag. I need you to come home."

"What? Why?"

"There are some things we need to discuss, and it's best done in person."

Kyle stood and rested his hand on Garrett's shoulder. Garrett's heart raced. What could Edward need to discuss with him that required him to fly all the way back to London?

"When are we talking about? We're kind of in the middle of a rather important project down here."

"I know, but this can't wait. I've already reserved you a seat on the eight-fifty flight tomorrow morning. You should be back on site within a week, in time for the start of the electrical rough-in."

Blast! He sighed and looked up at Kyle. Troubled blue eyes looked back at him. Garrett wrapped an arm around Kyle's waist and rested his forehead against Kyle's stomach. Kyle smoothed Garrett's hair, and the touch soothed some nerves jangling through him.

"I'll see you tomorrow."

He rang off and put his phone on the desk. Garrett stood, captured Kyle's face between his hands, and kissed him hungrily. He backed Kyle up against the wall, holding him where Garrett wanted. Kyle gripped the back of Garrett's head and tugged on his hair.

"What's wrong, *mon cheri*? Not that I mind the sensual assault, but you taste a little desperate."

Garrett rested his forehead against Kyle's then sighed. "I have to leave. Edward's already booked me for a flight first thing in the morning."

Kyle stiffened and pushed against Garrett's shoulders. "But you're coming back? Right?"

Garrett nodded. "He said a week, but I don't want to go." He stared into Kyle's eyes. "This is where I belong. With you. With Emir."

He took hold of Kyle, brushing their lips together, then doing it again. He loved how Kyle could switch from hard, demanding kisses to licking Garrett's lips softly before allowing their mouths to move together again and again in a way that made Garrett think they had all the time in the world to remain in just this spot. The kisses continued, gentle brushes of lips. However, Kyle held Garrett tight, his fingers digging into Garrett's arse cheeks with a fierce possessiveness.

Kyle smiled as he nipped at the soft spot beneath Garrett's chin. "Clearly, I've become attached to both of you, as demonstrated by my little tantrum earlier. But you'll be back before you realise it, and Emir and I will welcome you home in the best way possible."

"Think I can talk you into sending me off the same way?"

Kyle took another kiss and another. He moaned softly, searching for Kyle's groin with one hand, cajoling his lover into finishing what they'd started. Garrett knew he wouldn't have the same chance with Emir, and that almost made him even more desperate to be with Kyle. Almost as if by the two of them making love, he could feel Emir's presence in the trailer as well as he said goodbye. Kyle captured Garrett's hands and turned them so Garrett was pressed against the trailer wall, his hands pinned on either side of his head.

He shivered, trying to arch just a little closer. "Kyle..."

They broke the kiss. Kyle appeared as though he was contemplating Garrett's plea for several heartbeats longer than Garrett thought necessary, but then he sank to his knees in front of Garrett. Fresh air hit his skin as Kyle opened Garrett's trousers. His lover didn't even try to push them down or off, just wrapped warm, strong fingers around his cock.

"Bugger!" Garrett threw his head back, sinking his teeth into his bottom lip. "Ky!"

"You're like fire in my hand."

"Feels good, Ky." So much better than good. His hips jerked, pushing his cock into Kyle's wide palm.

"Hmm, only good?" Kyle squeezed a little.

"Bloody fucking brilliant."

"Then let's see what you think of my mouth."

Kyle teased Garrett's shaft with his lips, sliding around the crown, then down to his bullocks. Garrett reached out, hands connecting with the top of Kyle's head, not forcing but holding in place, as he swayed. Kyle flicked his tongue against the slit, tasting Garrett's essence. Another whimper caught in his throat.

He shivered, loving Kyle's touch as his thumbs stroked over Garrett's hipbones. Kyle pushed Garrett's trousers down around his legs, preventing him from spreading his legs.

"Love the way you smell. Like warm crème brûlée."

Slowly—oh, so slowly—Kyle's mouth closed around his knob. His cry could have rattled the thin walls of the trailer, the sensation almost enough to bring him to his knees. Kyle hummed, the vibrations echoing deep in Garrett's sac. Kyle pulled more of Garrett's cock in, lips tight and hot around him.

Blast! He would never hold it back. Garrett knew he was going to come so hard. Lightning bolts shot up and down his spine in rhythm with Kyle's bobbing head. His hips started rocking on instinct, head falling back to thunk against the panelled wall. Kyle slid his hands around to Garrett's ass, encouraging his movements.

"Going to... Can't..." Garrett pushed harder, faster, balls drawing up tight as marbles. Kyle tightened his grip, pulling him in, sucking his orgasm right out of him.

Garrett's knees shook and he slid down the wall to land in a heap on the hard floor, limbs splayed, limp as noodles. He slowly opened his eyes at Kyle's low chuckle.

"Give me five seconds to scoop my brains up and I'll return the favour."

"Not necessary."

Garrett frowned. Why would Kyle say something like that? He looked down to check the status of Kyle's cock, only to see spunk trailing down the slowly softening flesh and over Kyle's fingers. Garrett leaned forward and licked up the offering. Kyle's flavour on his tongue and the sound of his satisfied moan settled Garrett's rushing blood. He didn't know how he was going to get by for an entire week without his lovers.

For someone who'd put up a valiant, but foolhardy, resistance to succumbing to their attraction, Garrett was usually the one who sought Kyle's and Emir's touches several times a day. Now he was being forced to return to his solitary existence, and Garrett was less than enthusiastic about the situation.

Kyle snuggled up against Garrett after they had both adjusted their clothing to a more respectable status. "Want to try calling Emir again?"

If they weren't able to reach their lover, Garrett would have to leave without even saying goodbye. Emir would be with his family until late into the night. Most likely, he would go home to the flat over his workshop instead of coming to Garrett's. Kyle pulled his phone out of his pocket and Garrett read over his shoulder as Kyle typed out a text message to Emir, telling him to call as soon as he was able. All they could do now was wait. And Garrett would hope.

Chapter Seven

E mir looked around the crowded ballroom. He did not know how his parents, or, he supposed, his mother, had pulled off all the arrangements for this wedding in such a short amount of time. There had to be close to three hundred people in this room. Yet somehow, Emir knew the two most important people, in his opinion, were on the other side of the city. In a room full of people, their absences made Emir feel completely alone.

"Your sister looks beautiful."

"Yes, she does."

Emir looked over at the table where Kayra, Meriç and their witnesses sat. The ceremony by the government official had gone smoothly, and his baby sister was now a wife, which was a little odd considering he distinctly remembered the days she'd started crawling and walking, but she looked so happy that Emir could only enthusiastically celebrate her joy.

At the beginning of the day, his mother introduced Emir to the woman next to him. Her name was Nahla, and she was lovely, well spoken, and for all initial impressions, a genuine person. Too bad Emir had no interest in her beyond friendship. He glanced over at his parents, only to be speared with a look from his mother. Words weren't necessary for Emir to understand that his mother expected him to charm Nahla to the best of his abilities. They had already vetted her, and Emir's parents expected him to be the dutiful son and comply with their desires. Too bad for his parents that he believed in living his own life, not living his life for them.

Then again, if he really believed that, he might actually tell them the truth of his sexuality. But while he may not always agree with his parents, he respected them, love them. And the thought of seeing disappointment and disgust on their faces terrified him. Somewhere deep inside him still lived the little boy who craved his parents' smiles at the dawn of each new day.

Soon, a group of women would lead his sister away from the wedding table to assist her in changing from the contemporary Western white lace gown into a traditional Turkish wedding kaftan. Kayra had told him she'd picked a purple one with intricate gold embroidery, much to their mother's disappointment. Kayra had called Emir about a week ago and vented to him that if she got one more lecture on how a proper Turkish bride should behave, she was going to elope to Las Vegas. It had taken some time, but Emir had talked her away from the Expedia website.

As Kayra was being led from the table, Emir momentarily lost sight of her. However, right before she left the room, he caught sight of the red sash around her waist with the ribbons trailing down the skirt of her dress, a tradition amidst Turkish brides for good luck. He met Kayra's gaze and got a wink from his baby sister. He winked back.

"Your mother tells me you own a construction company and that you are building the next famous hotel."

He mentally cursed the woman who gave birth to him. "Not exactly. I own an architectural stone company. I design and install hand-carved and cut stone, but I don't do buildings. I do certain elements within and around a building."

Nahla frowned. "What do you mean?"

He pulled out his phone to show her some photos of his work and noticed that he'd missed several calls from Kyle and there was a text. He'd kept his phone on silent out of respect for the occasion, but he had thought he'd left it on vibrate. Apparently not. He clicked on the message and frowned.

"Is something wrong?"

He clicked away from the text quickly. "No, just a message from a friend. Let me show you some examples." He opened up his gallery and flipped through several photos. "Here are a couple of fireplaces surrounds I did for a client last year." He slid through several more photos and stopped at the shots he had taken when he'd worked on a restoration of a *yalı*, one of the historic waterfront homes on the Bosphorus. "These are some hand-carved columns I made."

"They're beautiful. You're a genuine artist, but why would your mother misspeak of your talents?"

He set his phone on the table and looked over at Nahla. He didn't want to encourage this hopeless situation, but his upbringing had instilled manners in him. "Because she wants me to meet a nice girl, settle down, and raise a family. She's decided that you're a suitable candidate. It's her opinion that if the woman believes her future husband can provide a comfortable existence, then she'll be more agreeable to the marriage. My parents firmly believe that what I do is an unstable way to make a living."

"Hmm, she must have been speaking to my father." She put her hand on Emir's forearm. "I, however, have other plans."

He let out a long breath and tried not to look too relieved.

Nahla smiled. "I think I'm getting the impression that you might as well." She looked into Emir's eyes closely. "Yes, in fact..." She glanced over at Emir's phone. "I think that message may be from someone who is more than a friend."

He stiffened and tried very hard not to stare at the phone, afraid that Kyle's or Garrett's smiling face might flash on the screen.

"She's a lucky girl, whoever she is. You're a very handsome and apparently talented man. I'm sure when you *are* ready, you'll make a wonderful husband and father."

His heart started beating again, and he smiled. Just because he was questioning his ability to maintain the secret of his sexuality for much longer didn't mean he was ready to be outed at a large family event.

"Thank you, and may I wish you all the best in your own plans."

Nahla leaned in conspiratorially. "I'll tell you a secret. I'm running away from home. My flight to the Maldives is all set. I recently finished a program in hotel management and I've received a job offer at the Four Seasons. I'm hoping to meet some nice island boys and enjoy some fun in the sand and sun."

Emir was about to respond when there was a loud cheer. He looked toward the crowd. His sister had reappeared, and she and Meriç made their way around the room. One tradition of Turkish weddings was that the bride and groom collected gifts of gold and money from their guests at the tables. It would be a little while before Kayra found her way over to Emir's table. He'd cashed in a savings bond, and while it wasn't a fortune, he hoped his gift would help Kayra and Meriç set up their new home.

After the gift gathering, Kayra would share a dance with their father. Then they would all enjoy the wedding feast, followed by the wedding cake Emir had been hearing about for the past three months.

At some point, he would need to call Kyle back. He didn't know what had his lover in such a twist. Both he and Garrett had known that today was the wedding and Emir would be busy all day. At least he assumed they'd remembered. Emir had told them on at least a couple of occasions. Kyle at least should have remembered, since the man had asked about coming more than once.

Emir wished he hadn't responded tersely to Kyle's requests, but he couldn't find a suitable way to express his fear to his lover—the man Emir was falling in love with. Scared that if he'd brought Kyle, even as a casual acquaintance and co-worker, someone would read their body language and expressions with enough astuteness to decipher their true relationship.

"Hello, brother."

Emir looked up and smiled at his sister. Her henna designs from *kini gecesi,* or the night of henna, were beautiful, the intricate and delicate images and patterns weaving up the back of her fingers, hands, and halfway up her forearms. The ink was burgundy red, the good luck colour of Turkey. She looked so grown up, and it suddenly hit him just how much he was going to miss her when she moved away.

Emir stood and pulled Kayra into his arms. *"Seni küçük kardeşi seviyorum."*

"I love you too. I need you to do something for me."

"Anything within my power. How can I refuse your request on today of all days?"

"Be happy, Emir." She looked over at Meriç and smiled. "I've found *bi tanem.* Yours is out there still waiting for you."

He looked over toward where he'd last seen his parents, but Kayra gripped his hand hard—harder than he'd thought a woman of her slight frame and stature was capable of.

"If you live for someone else's expectations, you'll always be a prisoner of your own making. Be free, brother."

She knew. Somehow, his sister had discovered his secret. Yet the love in her eyes wasn't only for her new husband. Emir swallowed hard and gave her the barest of nods. He eyed his phone, still sitting on the table. He needed to make a phone call. Emir reached into his jacket pocket and retrieved his gift.

"For your new home." He looked at Meriç and shook the man's hand. "Take good care of her."

"Always."

Kayra moved toward the dance floor. The lights of the ballroom dimmed, and their father walked out of the crowd circling the area. The sounds of drums, a dulcimer, and a wooden flute filled the air as Kayra and their father began a traditional Turkish folk dance.

Emir realised that he'd been neglecting his date since Kayra had re-entered the room. He turned to apologise, only to find that Nahla wasn't in the seat beside him anymore. He quickly scanned the room in search of her and saw that she was talking to a man near the dance floor. Nahla gave him a little wave and Emir knew he was off the hook for the rest of the evening.

Everyone's attention was on the dance floor, so Emir picked up his phone and walked toward the ballroom doors. He was about to call Kyle when his path became blocked—by his mother.

"Where are you going? Your sister's wedding feast is about to begin, and your date is alone!"

Whenever Emir heard his mother speaking rapid Turkish, memories of his childhood when he used to get scolded for trying to sneak sweets flashed through his mind.

"*Anne*, I don't think I've had the chance to tell you how beautiful you look tonight."

"Don't try to sweet talk me, Emir Şahin."

"I was simply stepping out to make a phone call. I will be right back."

"What could be more important than your sister's wedding celebration?"

Emir sighed. He wasn't sure if it was just the stress of the wedding, but lately his mother had been unusually high-strung. When Emir was growing up, she'd always been stern, but loving. Lately, though, Emir felt as though nothing he did was right.

"Maybe it has something to do with the *construction company* I own?"

Rana Şahin didn't appear the least bit apologetic for the lie.

"Why would you lie to Nahla?"

His mother waved off Emir. "It's not a true lie. You own a company that deals with construction. I was just trying to make sure the girl had a good first impression. The rest is up to you." She glanced around Emir's shoulder. "Although I might need to help with that too since she is currently speaking with a very handsome man..." She looked back at Emir and frowned. "Who is *not* my son."

Emir took his mother's hand and guided her over to a nearby table. His mother adjusted her kaftan, her dress and *hijab* more embellished than her typical everyday wear. At fifty-three, Rana Şahin's looks didn't suggest a year over forty—which, considering Emir was thirty-five, had made things awkward occasionally.

"*Anne*, I love you with all my heart. But you have to stop with the matchmaking."

"Why? What is wrong with Nahla? Your fathers have spoken, and both have expressed if the two of you suit, then negotiations can begin."

"*Anne*! You and father are *not* arranging my marriage—most especially without my consent." Emir stood and paced. He studied his mother. "I can't believe you even think such a thing is reasonable after all the times we've spoken about this."

"Sit down, Emir! You are making a scene."

Emir looked around. His raised voice caught the attention of a few nearby glances, but nearly all three hundred people present focused on the dance floor where Kayra and Meriç were sharing their first dance.

He sat, but his temper still boiled. "I know you and father had an arranged marriage, but what do I need to say to make you understand I will not let you choose who I will spend my life with?"

"What's wrong with Nahla?"

Emir felt like banging his head on the table. "Nothing is wrong with her. She's beautiful and kind, but neither of us is interested in anything more than friendship." He held up his hand to stop his mother's next words. "Do *not* say we'll find another girl."

In front of his eyes, his mother's typical commanding presence disappeared. "Why, Emir? What is preventing you from settling down? Why are you so opposed to the blessing of marriage? Did I do something wrong?"

Hearing the regret and confusion in his mother's voice, Emir felt his frustration drain away. She wasn't trying to be difficult. Her family had taught her from the time she was old enough to understand that being a good Muslim, building a home, and raising a family would be her role in life. She was simply trying to instil the same values in her children. Not that those were bad things, but both Emir and his sister had other goals. They were fortunate enough to live in a time when it was acceptable to blend traditional roles with modern lifestyles.

"No, *Anne*. Both Kayra and I consider ourselves very blessed to have you as our mother. It is not marriage I'm opposed to. It's..."Allah, could he do this? Here? Tonight of all nights? "It's..."

Rana lifted her hand to stop her son. "Say nothing else."

She glanced across the room to where people were making their way back toward their tables. When she looked back at Emir, her darkly lined eyes glistened with emotion.

"Tonight is for celebrating. Walk me to our table so the dinner can be served." She linked their arms and glanced up at Emir with a smile. "Although I have to say that what I'm really looking forward to is a piece of that cake."

Emir chuckled as the mother he was more familiar with reappeared. He was sure that the topic of his marriage, or lack thereof, would come up again. Someday, he would have to tell his parents the truth—especially if his relationship with Garrett and Kyle continued to grow stronger. His phone was a giant slab of limestone in his pants pocket, but he would find time to call his lovers sometime that night. He couldn't imagine not hearing their voices before he went to sleep.

Chapter Eight

Garrett mentally ran through his checklist one last time. His eyes were gritty and burned with exhaustion. The clock beside his bed read numbers that made him cringe when he thought of his alarm going off in just a few hours for him to catch his ride to the airport. He'd already arranged a transport service to the terminal. He'd checked his app to make sure the boarding pass was ready, and he'd sealed the zipper on his carry-on.

His heart hurt knowing that he wouldn't get the chance to connect with Emir before he had to leave. He'd tried calling his lover a couple of hours ago, but Emir hadn't answered—yet again. He was glad that Emir was enjoying his sister's wedding, but in all honesty, Garrett was a little gutted. How hard was it for Emir to pick up the phone and send a quick text acknowledging Garrett's and Kyle's repeated attempts to contact him?

He set his carry-on near the opening between the bedroom and the study. He stripped off his shirt and shucked his jeans. Strolling into the loo in nothing but his skivvies, he rubbed at his face. He could shave now to save time in the morning, but that would require more effort than he was willing to put out. After relieving himself, he brushed his teeth and slid on his sleep pants that hung over the heated towel rack. He loved slipping into warm flannels now that the nights were cooling.

As he left the loo, Garrett checked to make sure that all the lights were off in the flat. He clicked the switch on the wall just outside his bedroom, plunging the study into blackness. A loud bang suddenly echoed through the flat. Garrett just about fell arse over tit. The sound came again, and he realised it was someone banging on his front door. He looked over at the clock and the ridiculousness of the hour meant that either someone was there to kill him, or half the population of the United Kingdom had just spontaneously combusted and the King's Guard was there to inform him that Garrett was the new monarch. He really didn't think a killer would be polite enough to knock, so…

Garrett walked toward the door, stubbing his toe on his suitcase. He jumped down the hall, grabbing his toe and cursing. The pounding came again and now his blood pressure rose as he braced for a confrontation. Whoever stood behind that door was in for a rude greeting, King's Guard or not. He got the door and jerked it open.

"Piss off!"

Garrett found himself pushed backward against the wall.

Damn, it is the killer, after all.

A pair of firm lips covered his, and the scent of allspice hit his nose. A pair of brawny arms wrapped around him, and Garrett returned the embrace with a deep moan. He threaded his fingers through Emir's hair and held his lover's head in the best position to deepen the kiss. God, he loved how Emir was slightly bigger than he was, so he felt surrounded during times like this.

Emir pulled away from Garrett's lips, trailing kisses down his neck. "I only got the chance to check my messages after I left the hotel. I know it's late, but I couldn't let you leave without saying goodbye."

He wrapped his arms around Emir's waist and rested his head on his lover's shoulder. "No worries. I'm glad it's you and not a serial killer, though."

"What?"

"Never mind. Just kiss me again."

Emir took action, and Garrett succumbed to the strength of their passion. His lover tugged him away from the wall, and they started shuffling down the hall toward the bedroom. He wasn't sure if they'd make it unscathed, but nothing short of physical catastrophe was going to stop him from making love to his man.

They made it to the bed with all their limbs intact and only a few ricochets off the walls. Garrett landed on the mattress with Emir on top of him. Emir sat up, straddling Garrett's hips. He tugged on Emir's shirt, pulling the tails out of his trousers. Emir yanked the shirt open, buttons flying all over the room.

"Bloody hell, that's hot."

With his lover's chest revealed, Garrett let his fingers trace the multiple ridges and planes of smooth, dusky skin. Emir climbed off Garrett by sliding backward. He yanked Garrett's shorts off. He shivered and desire rushed through him as Emir slid his rough fingertips down his skin. Emir stripped off the rest of his clothing. Emir's cock captured Garrett's gaze as it hung full with arousal, the width and weight always filling Garrett to where his breath caught first in shock, then in sheer pleasure.

He stroked his hand up and down Emir's shaft. His lover moaned and Garrett's blood rushed a little faster, knowing that he could make such a magnificent man vulnerable. The mattress dipped further as

Emir knelt, bending over Garrett's cock. Emir opened his mouth and took the head of Garrett's dick inside.

He groaned and started thrusting in and out gently. He couldn't help it. Emir's mouth was so talented, and Garrett was always so thankful that the man genuinely loved sucking cock. The wet heat and powerful suction of Emir's mouth had Garrett groaning and his thighs tightening as he gripped the twisted covers beneath them.

"I'm going to come, but I want you inside me. Please, Emir. Don't let me leave empty."

"That is not an offer I will ever refuse."

He scooted farther back on the bed, Emir following him as they kissed over and over. Garrett loved missionary sometimes, but tonight he really needed a good, hard fuck. He needed to feel surrounded by his lover. He pushed at Emir and flipped himself over, waving his arse in invitation.

He gasped as a sharp crack rent the air, and a flash of pain flared from his arse. The pain quickly dissipated, and Garrett craved another slap. "Again. Please, again."

Emir complied, and Garrett's cock throbbed in response. He pushed his arse back into Emir's hand. He gripped his cock and squeezed, trying to hold off his orgasm until Emir got inside him.

"Hurry, love!"

There was the sound of the lube cap snapping open and a quick succession of Emir's fingers stretching Garrett's hole. It burned, but the ache was so perfect that he begged for more. Emir lined up behind him, then Garrett finally had his lover's thick cock pressing in until Garrett's body surrendered. He hissed while still pushing back for a deeper possession.

Emir stroked Garrett's back. "Easy, *canım*."

Garrett gave his body the time it needed to adjust, then flexed his channel as a signal. Emir was so good at reading Garrett's needs that he pulled back until just the tip of his cock was inside, then slammed back in. Garrett gripped his cock and jerked it even as he screwed himself on Emir's dick. The sounds of slapping flesh and harsh male groans filled the room. He begged Emir to take him harder and faster. Emir's grip on his hips was so strong that Garrett knew he'd be proudly wearing his lover's marks for the next several days while he was away. The bruises would serve as a reminder once the sensation of Emir filling him wore off.

Garrett's climax hit him so hard his vision blacked out and his bellow reverberated throughout the flat. Wave after wave of pleasure bombarded him. His muscles spasmed so hard he collapsed onto the mattress. Emir fucked him through every wave, pinning Garrett to the mattress and ploughing into him relentlessly until his rough roar joined Garrett's cries. Emir lay over Garrett, who was so blissed out he didn't even care that there was a huge wet spot beneath him.

Eventually, Emir's cock softened, and he withdrew, causing Garrett to groan. Garrett rolled over, his body humming with pleasure and his well-used muscles trembling with the residual echoes of their lovemaking. A cool cloth wiped across his stomach, causing Garrett to suck in a quick breath. Emir tugged and turned them until they lay under the covers. Garrett curled into Emir's embrace, cataloging the sensation for the long, empty nights ahead of him back in his homeland.

Garrett walked into the lobby of the world headquarters of Totally Five Star Hotels. He waved to Paul, the security guard.

"Mr Sloan! Great to see you. I didn't know you were back in town."

"Just for a few days, then I have to get back."

"Well, if you don't mind me saying so, it seems Turkey agrees with you. If I didn't know better, I'd think you've been vacationing in Fiji or something."

Garrett smiled. "Thanks. I suppose my pasty British skin has darkened a few shades, but don't tell Mr. Conroy that or he'll think we're wasting all his money on Turkish sweets and tea."

Paul chuckled and acted as if he was zipping his lips closed. Garrett waved as he crossed over to the bank of lifts. The heels of his dress shoes clacked on the marble floors. He adjusted his tie. This was the first time he'd worn a suit in a couple of months. It was amazing how he'd forgotten how constrictive the things were.

Garrett glanced up when the lift tone signalled the car's arrival. He stepped inside and pushed the button for the twenty-fifth floor. Before Garrett had a chance to adjust his cuff links one last time, the lift slowed, bounced to a stop, and the doors opened. He stepped out and the thick carpet cushioned his steps as he walked toward the reception desk. He waved to Jinelle and headed down the hall in the direction of his office. As he passed the other executive offices, it was nice to see familiar faces.

He glanced at his watch and saw that it was almost half past twelve. Edward had told Garrett to come by his office as soon as he arrived at the building. Garrett hadn't even taken the time to go home before coming in. He rolled his carry-on into his office and set it against the wall, then he took out his phone and sent a quick text to Emir and Kyle, letting them know he'd arrived safely.

His body still had deep vibrations from Emir's lovemaking earlier that morning. It was too bad Kyle hadn't been there too, but when he got back to Istanbul, Garrett would track down both his lovers and show them just how thankful he was that they cared enough to say goodbye.

Garrett looked around his office and, for some reason, almost felt like a visitor. He glanced at his credenza and saw photographs of his family and past projects. The walls displayed his degree certificate from Oxford. It wasn't as if Garrett was unfamiliar with travel, either. Since he'd become director of operations five years ago, he spent just about as much time in the field as he did in the office, frequently spending months at a time in one exotic country or another. Yet for some reason, this time, London didn't feel like coming home.

"Hello, Garrett."

He turned and saw his boss in the doorway. "Hello. I was just on my way to your office."

"Well, then I saved you a long trip down a short hall. How was your flight?"

"The usual." Garrett walked over to the compact refrigerator beneath the countertop of his bar. He opened it and smiled when he saw the sparkling water he'd been anticipating since he'd landed in London. He removed the green bottle, twisted the cap open, then took a big drink. "God, I've missed this stuff."

Edward smirked. "Never understood how you could stand it myself. I made reservations at Les Deux Salons for lunch. If we want to get there on time, we'll need to leave in the next few minutes."

Garrett recapped his bottle and put in back in the mini-fridge. "I'm ready."

During the entire cab ride to the restaurant, Garrett was trying to read Edward's mood. Why had his boss made him fly fifteen hundred miles on less than twenty-four hours' notice? Certainly it wasn't for lunch. As far as he knew, the company wasn't in danger of going under or being sold. Edward didn't seem to be upset, so Garrett didn't think he'd done anything wrong or was in jeopardy of being sacked. Then again, they probably wouldn't be heading toward an upscale restaurant if Garrett was about to be given his card. All the conjecture in the world wouldn't help him discover the answers. Edward would reveal his reasons when he was bloody well ready.

Frustrating little sod.

They exited the cab and headed into the restaurant. Garrett and Edward had eaten here before. He typically ordered the grilled tiger prawns, which sounded rather delicious after his flight. Despite the busy atmosphere, Edward's table reservation ensured they were seated immediately. As Garrett crossed the tiled floor, he thought of all the mosaics in Istanbul. He'd become so used to the colourful designs that the black and white of the elegant French restaurant seemed dull, despite the geometric design. They occupied a corner booth that granted them a little privacy, unlike some of the other tables where separate parties sat almost elbow to elbow.

The hostess placed the menus in front of them. Garrett glanced at the special of the day, but decided he'd stay with his usual. He waited impatiently as Edward studied the offerings. Garrett sipped his water and people-watched. Most of the diners appeared to be professionals. More black and grey suits filled the chairs than Garrett had seen in seven months. Once again, he compared his homeland to Istanbul and again, found it rather dreary.

"So, I imagine you're chewing at the bit trying to figure out why I ordered you back home."

"I'd be lying if I said no. So why don't you put me out of my misery?"

"I should make you suffer through lunch, just because I can, but that would ultimately only be a disservice to my own interests."

Garrett stared his friend and boss down. He wouldn't allow himself to be lured into Edward's taunts.

"I'm retiring."

Garrett's heart stopped for several beats and the air locked in his chest.

"Breathe, Sloan. This is a good thing."

"Of course. I'm sorry. You simply surprised me. I kind of thought you'd be one of those who died at your desk."

"Hmm. Yes, well, if I don't slow down, that might become a reality. And I'd much rather spend my silver years as a doddering old fool trying to figure out what latest craze my grandkids are blathering on about."

Garrett leaned forwards, frowning. "What's going on, Ed? When I left for Istanbul, you were planning projects for the next five years."

"I had a bit of an... episode last month. My doctor said that if I don't slow down, I would be forced to—permanently."

"Jesus. So you're stepping down. Who's taking your place?"

"I have a shortlist of candidates."

Their lunch arrived, and Garrett set his napkin across his lap. He used the few moments to hide the slight tremble of his hands. He couldn't believe Edward was retiring. Garrett had only been partially joking when he had said that his boss would be one of those who died at their desk. The man had been Garrett's mentor during university when he earned a work placement with Totally Five Star Hotels. After earning his bachelor's degree, they'd recruited him for an entry-level position. While many of Garrett's school friends had moved from one company to another every few years, he'd never had a reason to seek another position. The company had always treated him well, and his co-workers, mostly, had been congenial. It looked like things were going to change.

"Well, please let me know if there's anything you need from me during the interview process."

"There is one thing." Edward took a bite of his crab and avocado salad. He sat back in his chair and smiled. "I want you to take my job."

Garrett choked on his bite of prawn. He coughed into his napkin. His eyes watered. He took a drink of water, followed by another. "I..." He coughed again and waved off the server, who was looking at their table with concern. "I thought you said you had a shortlist?"

"It's very short."

"I'm honoured that you would consider me for a promotion of such significance, but do you mind if I ask why?"

"Garrett, you've worked your arse off for this company for twenty bloody years. Every division you've worked in has shown an increase in production. Since you became director of operations, every project you've headed up has come in not only on time, but under budget, too. Well except for this one, and I think we can safely say that was not your doing. Your projects have turned record profits for our company because guests keep coming back. And every review, we receive comments on the quality of facilities and experience based on the atmosphere of the design."

"Well, that had more to do with the architects who design the buildings and the managers and staff who operate them, not my ability to manage the construction process."

Edward set his utensils on the table and sighed. "Somehow, I expected a more enthusiastic response to this offer." Call me batty, but now that you and LaFleure are together, I thought the idea of not having to travel around the world and be away for months on end might be appealing."

Garrett lifted his napkin from his lap and placed it over his unfinished lunch. He couldn't eat another bite. "It is. And I'm honored, but if I take over the chief operating officer position then..."

"Talk to me, Garrett."

"Kyle and I are together, but there's someone else."

"You're cheating on LaFleure? I have to say I never thought you'd be the type of man to go behind another's back."

Garrett shook his head and glanced around to see if any of the other diners had overheard Edward's exclamation. "No. No. I mean, we have a third. A Turkish man."

"Oh. Really? How does that...? Never mind, I don't want to know. Tell me one thing, though. What do you plan on doing when you finish the project in Istanbul? You and Kyle planned to return to the UK, anyway."

"We haven't talked about it. Our third owns a business in Turkey. A very renowned one. He has contacts all over the world and clients who seek his services. He has lived his whole life in Istanbul and all his family is there. We've just been..."

"Living in the moment? Riding the wave of a new relationship?"

"I suppose so."

"And if you take my job offer, the bubble will burst and you'll have to face some hard decisions."

"The decisions will come whether or not we want them to. This is more than casual between the three of us. Your offer is simply forcing us to ask questions much sooner than I think we're prepared to do. Although I have to say, I'm a bit surprised by your apparent apathetic response to my announcement."

Edward shrugged. "I won't pretend to understand the compulsion to have multiple partners, but I also don't understand the biology behind same sex attraction. Frankly, I don't care to know what happens in your bedroom, but I consider you a friend. And as my friend, I want you to be happy. And as your boss—for at least the time being—I want you to be productive on the job. If sharing your life with two men will help achieve that, then... *C'est la vie.*"

"For argument's sake, how do you see this transition happening?"

"There's the shrewd businessman I know. I plan to cut back on my responsibilities over the course of the next year. My replacement—who I'm still hoping is the man sitting across from me—will take over those duties, and when I feel it's safe for me to step down without too much upheaval to the company, I will. I've already spoken with the CEO and he's in full support of the plan."

Garrett chuckled. "I should hope so, considering you've spent the past forty-five years turning Totally Five Star Hotels into the international success it is today. Well, that and I suppose because he's your godson, his father's best friend, and doesn't want you to die of a stroke or something."

Edward smiled. "It has been quite a journey. And now I'd like to spend the time I have left enjoying the rewards of working so hard."

"Give me some time to think things over? A chance to talk to my partners? I will have an answer for you by the end of the week."

"No, you won't, because we have planned for the rest of your time here to be dedicated to meetings. Our research department has already started field studies on the proposed locations for the next project. We feel as though we've found a great niche in the luxury accommodations market with the concept of designs that assimilate their environment. I'll give you till the end of the month to make your decision."

Bloody hell, how am I supposed to choose between what is possibly the love of a lifetime and the realisation of a dream I've spent twenty years in preparation for? Especially when both feed my soul.

Chapter Nine

Kyle stood in the middle of *sıcaklık,* or hot room, of the new *hamam.* Today, the workers would install the marble slabs throughout the room. Kyle had learned that one of the critical elements of an authentic *hamam* was the use of marble for all the surfaces in the hot room. Not only was it tradition, but the solid surface material was seen as pure and cleansing.

Initially, they'd tasked Emir with fitting out the *hamam,* but with the three interconnecting spaces, the scale of the project was simply too much for one person. Instead, they'd contracted the bulk of the work with the company Kyle had consulted for the *hamam* design. The marble slabs, tiles, and fixtures were coming from their warehouse. But Emir designed the medallion for the *göbektaşı,* or heated slab, where guests would relax, lie, work up a sweat and get their soap massages. He had also designed and carved the *kurna,* or basin, which would hold the water the attendants would use to rinse the guests after their scrub massages on the raised platforms placed in a few strategic points around the perimeter of the room. Unlike regular basins with drains, the design of the *kurna* called for the water to run over the edges in a continuous flow. When Kyle had been at Emir's workshop yesterday, his lover had shown him the finished project. The details of the fountains were stunning. He knew Emir had carved the stone by hand and the designs had simply come from his mind. The display had really forced Kyle to realise the extent of Emir's talent.

Kyle studied the six interior arches held up by Corinthian columns, also designed by Emir, which circled the interior of the room and supported the dome. He moved through an arch into the centre and looked up at the dome that curved six meters over his head. Sunlight came through the star-shaped cutouts, creating beams of light that crisscrossed the chamber. The space, once finished, will have a stunning effect. Kyle might work with a computer aided drafting program, but in a way, this project had proven to him he was capable of artistry as well. The hotel design had really challenged him to be innovative, and he was convinced it was the best work he'd ever done.

They built a low bench into the exterior wall around the entire area. The kurna would be installed along that wall. And behind each *kurna,* they would install the tiled and carved back decores. There were two arched doors that connected the hot room to both the reception and the cool rooms. Over the centre of the *göbektaşı,* a Mediterranean styled bronze and glass globe chandelier would eventually hang.

"*Aşkim,* what are you doing?"

Kyle turned to look at Emir. He dressed as normal on the worksite, but Kyle knew the poetry of his lover's body beneath the sturdy clothing. Last night, Emir had stayed at Kyle's flat. They'd fallen asleep in pure exhaustion shortly after supper, but Emir had woken Kyle with the most tender of touches and made love to him in a way that had left Kyle floating in a haze of pleasure for hours.

"Taking inventory of the shipment. The installers should be here soon. Are you sure you want to spend the day taking orders from them?"

Emir walked closer to Kyle and put his arms around his waist. He bent and kissed Kyle quickly. "Taking orders has never been a problem for me. I was a soldier, after all. But that is not important. In truth, I've been looking forward to this part of the project since Garrett contacted me. While I am very grateful that Garrett didn't assign me the complete design and responsibility for supplying all the materials, I still very much want to be involved in the installation process."

Kyle kissed Emir's neck, inhaling his lover's natural scent. "*Bon*. I just wanted to make sure."

They separated and Kyle crossed to a large crate in the corner, stepping over the rows of PEX tubing covering the subfloor that was part of the radiant heating system. Inside the crate were large, square marble tiles for the floor that would be the first thing installed. They would tile the exterior walls in marble as high as the peak of the interior arches, which was about three meters.

Right now, everything looked so rough with pipes poking out of the wall and the PEX tubing snaking all over the floor—not to mention periodic holes for the duct work of the HVAC system—but Kyle could picture the end product in his head.

"While I'm in here working up a sweat, what are you going to do?"

Kyle spun around and saw Emir leaning against one of the marble columns. *Merde, he looks sexy.* "I'll be checking in with the electrician in the guest suite area. They're finishing the rough-in so we can start dry-walling tomorrow. You know, sometimes I wanted to rip this tablet out of Garrett's hands, but since he's been gone, I think my palm has permanently moulded to its shape."

Emir smiled. "*Evet*, I know what you mean. However, you've done an admirable job filling in for Garrett."

"*Merci*, but when he comes back, I'll be thrilled to relinquish this thing," he said, holding up the tablet.

"Have you spoken with him today?"

Kyle shook his head. "He said he'd be in meetings all day, but..."

Emir pushed away from the column and came toward Kyle. "What is it, *aşkım*? What has you frowning?"

"I didn't realise how much I would miss him. When he told me he had to leave, I had a moment of panic, then chastised myself because I knew he'd be back. It's not as if Garrett would willingly walk away from this project, not after all the hard work we've done over the past couple of years. I figured, what's a few days?" He looked up at Emir and smiled. "Besides, I've got you. *Oui*?"

"*Evet*, you have me. But I'm not a substitute for Garrett. He's a part of this... thing we've created, and with him gone, it's only right we both feel his absence."

"You miss him too?"

Emir nodded. "Of course I do. It's only been two weeks, but each day that goes by and I don't get the chance to look into his green eyes or kiss his firm lips makes the tiny hole in my heart widen. I've enjoyed this time we've had together, but I also feel guilty because I have enjoyed myself when I know that he's all alone."

Hearing his own thoughts coming from Emir's lips, shock reverberated through Kyle. The past two weeks had really helped Kyle get to know his Turkish lover better. He'd been so surprised when Emir had willingly shared parts of his life that Kyle thought extremely private—including his frustration with his family and the stress he felt from the pressure of their expectations. So, last night, he'd lain in Emir's arms feeling guilty because Garrett's absence had allowed the two of them the opportunity for such intimacy, and in a way, he was glad for it.

"Hopefully, he'll be back at the end of the week. Then the three of us can have some quality time together. Maybe we should get away for a weekend. I've heard of a place in Cappadocia where they've turned some caves in a hillside into a luxury resort. I'd love to see it."

"Ah, the Kayakapi. I did some work with them during the restoration."

"Really? That's fantastic. Now we have to go."

Emir chuckled, giving Kyle a kiss. "Okay, *aşkım*, I'll contact the owners, since they are good friends, and make some arrangements. We'll have to get a suite, so there is no suspicion of our relationship."

Kyle didn't like it, but he knew such things were a reality in this part of the world. It didn't matter. He knew that once darkness fell, he, Emir and Garrett would all be in one bed, sharing one another's bodies as their hearts became more and more entwined.

Kyle took a sip of wine, eyeing Emir across the small round table in his tiny kitchen. They'd gone back to Kyle's flat after finishing at the construction site for the day. Emir seemed a little distracted, but Kyle could tell he was reluctant to talk. In fact, they'd hardly said anything since they sat to the dinner Emir had prepared. Kyle didn't mind the silence. It was comfortable, but if there was something Emir needed to talk about, Kyle wanted his lover to know that he was available.

"Everything okay, *mon coeur*?"

"*Evet*. I'm sorry I'm poor company tonight."

Kyle placed his hand on Emir's and smiled. "You're never poor company. I can see, however, that you're deep in thought about something. I'm here if you need to talk."

Emir stood and walked over to Kyle's side of the table. He bent over, put his hand on the back of Kyle's neck, and kissed him. Kyle closed his eyes and held onto Emir's arm. He pushed his way out of the chair and turned Emir so that he was up against the wall. Emir might have been taller and stronger than Kyle, but his lover willingly let Kyle take charge.

Hmm, maybe my Turkish heart needs some special loving tonight?

Kyle gasped when Emir squeezed him tightly, practically cutting off his air supply. He petted and kissed up and down Emir's neck, whispering soothing words of encouragement.

"I think you need one of my special massages to help you relax. *Oui?*"

Emir nodded, and Kyle saw him blinking his eyes and swallowing hard. Whatever was bothering his lover really had him torn up. No matter. Kyle would take care of everything. By the end of the night, Emir would be a pile of relaxed goo.

He took Emir's hand and led him to the bedroom. The hardwood floors beneath their feet creaked slightly. Kyle's place was a historic building in Galata. It had some nice architectural details, such as hardwood floors, high ceilings and exposed brick. However, it was a lot smaller than Garrett's. Most importantly, his bed was only a double, which was why the three of them spent most of their time together in the Cihangir flat overlooking the Bosphorus.

Kyle left the overhead light off and turned on only the bedside lamp. He set his phone on the dresser and started some soft instrumental Turkish music. Kyle had really learned to enjoy the folk music of Emir's homeland. He guided Emir over to the bedside and the two of them worked on stripping the barriers between their flesh. The whole time, Kyle used every opportunity to touch Emir—touches meant to soothe and relax.

"Lie down, face up. I'm going to get the massage oil."

Kyle noticed that Emir's gaze followed him the entire way to the bedside table. He retrieved the oil, along with a condom and some lube.

He saw Emir smile and shrugged. *"Quoi? J'ai pensé pourquoi bousculade quand vient le temps."*

Emir frowned, and Kyle realised that he'd reverted to French. The three of them had found that English worked best for communication. Garrett knew a fair amount of French, and Emir a few basics. Garrett had picked up some Turkish since being in the country, but not enough for detailed conversation. Kyle, on the other hand, was struggling with the complex language. Emir spoke very good English, even if his language was a bit formal. So they'd found that there was a lot less confusion if they stuck with that, although sometimes one or another of them would slip up.

He sat on the bed, then straddled Emir's hips. He dribbled some oil into the palm of his hand, then rubbed them together. Emir's cock was still soft, but Kyle had a feeling that was going to change. He loved the hefty weight nestled between his ass cheeks, even soft.

"Sorry. I said why scramble when it comes time?" he said, placing his slick hands on Emir's smooth chest and massaging in circular motions. "But first, we need to loosen all these tight muscles and get those stress lines off your face."

He used long strokes, moving toward Emir's heart to stimulate blood flow. He worked Emir's chest and shoulders. When Emir closed his eyes and sighed, Kyle felt his lover relax. Kyle worked on Emir's arms next. He picked up Emir's hand and used his thumbs to dig into his lover's palm, the skin somewhat rough from the manual labour involved with Emir's job. Emir moaned, and Kyle felt Emir's cock flex beneath his ass. He repeated the same treatment to the other side.

He lifted and scooted down the bed, moving to the side so he wouldn't have to shift around again and disturb Emir. Kyle studied Emir's body. Even in his lover's relaxed state, every muscle was chiselled to perfection. Emir wasn't a bulky man, but he was strength personified.

He focused on Emir's legs. As he rubbed the inside of Emir's thighs, Kyle noticed Emir getting hard. The temptation to stroke the thick cock in front of him was extremely strong, but he knew they would eventually progress to sexual activity. Kyle added more oil to his hands and started massaging Emir's calf. He hit a knotted area and focused his touch on that spot until he felt the knot pop. Emir groaned, then sighed. Kyle repeated his treatment to the other leg.

"It's time to roll over."

Emir adjusted himself until he was comfortable. *"Seni durdurmak asla yalvarıyorum."*

"I have no idea what you just said, but I'm hoping it wasn't 'stop, you're hurting me'."

"Hayir."

Kyle chuckled. "Now that one I know. Don't worry, *mon coeur*, I'm going to take good care of you."

He re-oiled his hands. He started on Emir's back, moving down as he had on the front side. When Kyle reached Emir's ass, he paid particular attention to the taut globes. He dribbled some oil in Emir's crack and used his thumbs to slide up and down the trench, circling his hole in soft strokes with just enough pressure so that Emir recognised his intent. In the last seven months, Emir had only bottomed twice.

Once for Garrett and once for Kyle. Now Kyle was going to have his second chance to be inside his Turkish heart.

Emir curled his arms around a pillow, turning his head to one side. Kyle swore he saw a little smile on Emir's lips. He nudged Emir's thighs apart. If he was going to have this opportunity, he was going to make the absolute best of it.

Kyle looked down at the dark rose of Emir's skin. He practically drooled. Kyle used his thumbs to part Emir's cheeks, exposing his back entrance. "I'm going to taste you everywhere."

Emir lifted his ass, silently asking for Kyle's tongue. Kyle bent over and licked softly up and down Emir's crack. He flicked the tip of this tongue across and around Emir's opening, exploring all the textures of the tight ring of muscle. The more Kyle feasted on Emir's asshole, the more the man writhed and moaned under the workings of his mouth.

"No one has ever... It feels so..."

Emir's words had Kyle redoubling his efforts. Knowing that he was the first man ever to give his lover this sensation had Kyle's desire soaring to new heights. He pushed more and more with his tongue against Emir's hole. The tip of his tongue breached Emir's asshole, and he wiggled it back and forth.

"Ahhh, *Evet!*"

That was the response Kyle had been hoping for. He pushed farther in, using his tongue to fuck Emir as his lover continued to writhe beneath him. Kyle picked the lube up off the bed and released the cap with a flick of his thumb. Emir's moans drowned out the snap in the room. As the cool gel hit his fingertips, Kyle shivered in anticipation. He pulled his mouth away from Emir's ass, placed a finger against the now pliant ring of muscle, and pushed inward. Emir took one finger fairly easily since he was so relaxed, so Kyle added another. Slowly, he stretched him, taking the time to rub against Emir's gland every few strokes.

Emir gloried in the feeling of Kyle's fingers inside him, but he needed more. He needed their bodies to be locked in the most intimate way possible. *"Ihtiyacım var lütfen,"* he said, softly.

"All right, roll to your side."

Emir followed Kyle's instructions and lifted his top leg to open his body farther. The heat from Kyle behind him made Emir's muscles stay relaxed, even if he was slightly nervous.

Kyle adjusted their bodies. Since Emir had a few inches on Kyle in height, his lover's lips rested on the curved of his shoulder. There was pressure against his entrance as Kyle positioned himself, and Emir had a moment of trepidation. He knew there would be pain since he didn't do this often, but experience had proved that once he had one of his lovers inside him, only pleasure would remain. Right now, the most important thing was to become one with Kyle.

The mushroom head of Kyle's cock nudged forward, breaching Emir. Kyle didn't have the width that Emir did, or quite the length of Garrett, but his lover was—in Emir's opinion—a perfect size. Emir let out a long breath and tried to relax as Kyle slowly sank inside him. He lifted his leg farther, opening himself up even more to the shaft, sinking into his ass. It may have been Kyle's body entering him, but Emir felt the possession more in his heart.

He loved Kyle and Garrett. There was no purpose to denying his feelings other than to save public face and spare his family the turmoil of disgrace. Emir let out another long groan as Kyle's cock impaled him fully. The sting of Kyle's entry faded to a slight throb of pleasure. He felt his body accepting Kyle's cock more and more with each passing second. Kyle latched his firm lips onto the sensitive junction between Emir's neck and shoulder, sucking on the skin. Emir didn't know if it was enough to leave a mark, but he didn't care either way. Kyle reached over Emir's hip and took his cock in hand.

Emir relaxed his neck and let his head fall back. He let out a cry as Kyle pulled his dick out slowly, then sank in again with a bit more force. Each time Kyle withdrew, Emir felt his sphincter clamp down, holding his lover inside him. His body was so sensitised by the combination of Kyle's lips, cock and hand that Emir felt as though every nerve ending crackled with static electricity. Kyle slowly circled the tip of Emir's cock with his thumb, flicking across the slit that wept with pleasure. Every surge of Kyle's cock inside him stroked Emir's prostate, pushing him closer to that edge.

He vaguely heard Kyle whispering in French his ear, but Emir didn't have the ability nor did he care to understand the words. The tone and timbre of his lover's voice were enough for Emir to get the point. There were some things in life that didn't need interpretation.

Kyle thrust into him at a depth and angle that provided the most direct stimulation to his gland. Kyle intensely stroked Emir's cock with his large hand. Emir teetered on the edge of oblivion. It was so close, but he just couldn't...

His lover gently bit down on the stretched tendon of his neck and it all became too much. Emir came with a shout, everywhere—on his chest, his chin—and his orgasm surged through every living cell of his body, renewing the vitality of life within him.

Kyle continued to thrust into him, clearly lost to the power of his own pleasure. Kyle gripped Emir's hip and pushed him over slightly. The change in position sent Kyle's cock plunging into him deeper. Unbelievably, his body responded. Though he knew he wouldn't get hard again so quickly, the sheer energy being fed to him through Kyle's lovemaking extended Emir's pleasure to heights previously unknown.

Emir gripped the sheets beneath him. French and Turkish words blended in the air, the sound more beautiful than any music he'd ever heard. Just as Emir's vision darkened around the edges and his ears rang, Kyle froze deep inside him. Emir felt Kyle's cock throb with each jet of his release.

"Je t'aime, mon coeur turc!" Kyle shouted.

"Seni seviyorum," Emir whispered.

Chapter Ten

Kyle walked out of the last guest suite after doing a walk-through of the rough electrical with the electrician and general contractor. The task had fallen to him when Garrett had got delayed by a couple of weeks of work in London.

"Everything looks great. I really appreciate your team working overtime the last couple of days, so we can stay on schedule."

"We made a commitment."

He shook the hand of the general contractor. He was a man of few words, but knew his stuff and worked hard. Because of the scope of the project, Garrett had decided to complete everything by zones. The *hamam* had been zone one because of the extensive finish work required for the space. Zone two included the guest suites. The restaurant and kitchen were zone three. Common areas such as the lobby, fitness room, lounge and business centre would be the last areas to be finished out on the main floor. The lower level contained the laundry service area, employee locker rooms, utility management areas, and so forth.

In the time Garrett had been gone, the hotel had turned from an empty shell of a building into something actually resembling a habitable structure. Monday, the electrician's team would report to the restaurant and the insulation and drywall crew would begin work on the guest suites. Emir and the other installers had been working on setting all the marble in the *hamam's sıcaklık*, or hot room, for the past week. They still had to complete all the tile work in the *soğukluk*, or cool room, and the *camekan*, or welcome hall. They expected they would need at least another three weeks to complete everything. Then they had to construct the private dressing cubicles, assemble the chaises lounges in the cool room and eight hundred million other things.

He looked down at the tablet, and his eyes swam. "I hate this job! How in the fucking hell does Garrett do this and not go mental?" He scanned the delivery schedule. "Shit, I forgot to verify the order for the electric supplies in the restaurant. *Bon sang je souhaite que Britt sanglante serait revenir.*"

"Sounds like this bloody Brit got back just in time."

He jerked his head up. "Garrett," he whispered. "*Mon coeur!*"

He ran toward Garrett's open arms. The moment his Brit's arms came around him, all the tension that had been living in Kyle's muscles melted away. He tightened his grip and sighed when Garrett rested his lips on the side of Kyle's neck for a couple of seconds before they separated.

"Missed you," Garrett whispered.

"Oh, God, me too. Us, I mean. Me and Emir. We both did. So much."

Garrett chuckled. "Well, I hope it was you and Emir. I don't know anybody else who would miss me."

He looked around, then angled Garrett down for a kiss. It was the first time their lips had touched in three weeks. Kyle couldn't breathe.

He was afraid to make the slightest move in case it broke the spell and Garrett stopped. How had he ever resisted this man for over a year? The past weeks had been hell in some ways. Even though he revelled in the light kiss, Kyle wanted more. The desire to pin Garrett up against a stud, cuff his hands above his head in one of his wrists and plunder his mouth was very strong.

He became more insistent, using his tongue and lightly nudging Garrett's lips apart. Garrett opened up to him, readily accepting Kyle's possession, even returning Kyle's kiss with eagerness. He wrapped his arms around his lover. The solid warmth of Garrett enveloped him, and Kyle's cock hardened against his Brit. Kyle refused to relinquish the kiss as he slid his hands up and down Garrett's back, then he pushed them beneath Garrett's suit coat until he clutched the dress shirt beneath. He pulled the shirt from Garrett's slacks. He felt Garrett tense, then break the kiss.

"I'm sorry." Kyle rested his head against Garrett's, panting. "This isn't the place, but—"

"Bloody fuck, I needed that."

He kissed Garrett softly. "I think we both got a little carried away. Why don't we go rescue Emir and then go back to your place?"

"That's the best proposal I've heard since I left." Garrett looked around the floor. "What did you do with my tablet?"

He had no idea. The moment Garrett's lips had touched his, he had forgotten all about the cursed thing. He saw the thin black rectangle lying on a pile of drywall close to the floor-to-ceiling window. "There," he said, pointing.

Garrett picked up the computer and brushed it off. "It looks like no harm came to it."

Kyle growled. "Your arrival allowed it a stay of execution."

Garrett laughed and put his arm around Kyle. "Oh, come now. It's just a helpful piece of technology. You wouldn't believe how much easier this has actually made my job."

He shuddered, then turned and stopped Garrett in his tracks. "Just don't leave me alone again, please."

"I won't. I promise."

He had meant his words to refer to Garrett's responsibilities on the construction site, but as he looked into Garrett's jewel-coloured eyes, he saw that Garrett's response had a much deeper meaning. Was it possible that Garrett's feelings for him and Emir had deepened, despite his absence?

They left the rear wing of the hotel and walked down the hall toward the *hamam* complex. The hallways already had drywall installed and were mudded. So, as they made their way down the corridor, lines and blobs of drywall mud served as decoration. Eventually, they would paint the walls and tile the ceilings, but that wouldn't happen until later.

Garrett stopped suddenly and Kyle turned to see what had caught his attention. They stood in the middle of the hallway with the arched doorways of the restaurant on one side and the rear wing of the Bosphorus view suites on the other.

"Wow," Garrett whispered. "I knew. I'd seen all the drawings, the models, even stood in this very spot before I left, but I didn't understand. Not really." He turned to look at Kyle. "You are a genius—both you and Emir. Just look at those columns."

It was pretty dramatic. Three and a half meter high limestone columns stood on either side of the two openings, mirroring each other. Emir had hand-carved Turkish designs into each of the pillars. Kyle watched as Garrett walked over to the columns and traced the patterns. Kyle knew that each pillar had taken Emir a month to carve.

They were some of the first items their lover had done after signing on to the project.

"Just wait until you see the fountain for the courtyard."

Quickly, Garrett looked over at Kyle. "He finished it?"

Kyle nodded. "He's spent the last week in his workshop at night after we finished here. He showed it to me this morning, and... There are no words. You just have to see for yourself."

"You guys have been busy."

Kyle blinked and looked away. He wasn't sure how Garrett felt about the time he and Emir had spent alone. He didn't want to rub it in Garrett's face, but at the same time, Kyle wasn't about to deny how much closer he and Emir had become. How they'd confessed their love for each other. To do so not in Garrett's presence seemed cruel.

Garrett put his arms around Kyle's waist and held him. "Hey. What's going on inside your head? Why the quick avoidance?"

"What did you mean by that?"

"By what? You two being busy? Just that. This place looks amazing. It's come so far in the three weeks I've been gone."

"So you weren't making some reference to the time Emir and I have had alone? You're not jealous?"

Garrett stepped away. "Is that what you think? First, of course I'm jealous." Kyle spun around and opened his mouth, but Garrett held up his hand. "Not in a bad way, though. Look, the three of us will never spend equal amounts of time with one another. If we keep score, then it's only going to lead to resentment. Would I love to spend some one-on-one time with you? With Emir? Absolutely. But does that mean I want to get rid of one of you to achieve that? Never."

"I'm sorry. I guess we're still trying to figure all this out, aren't we?"

The soft kiss he received went a long way toward soothing the ire that had quickly flashed inside him.

"Hmm, but we're having fun along the way. Now take me to our Turk. I want to see what he's been up to."

Kyle smiled. "Come on."

He took Garrett's hand, and they headed down the hall of the rear guest wing. On one side were the fifteen arched door openings. On the other were three glassed doorways leading to the courtyard. There were matching doorways on all four sides of the courtyard leading from various parts of the hotel. They turned to go down the hallway on the opposite side of the building from where they had started.

He paused at the opening of what would eventually be the door to the *hamam* welcome hall. "Are you ready?"

Garrett nodded and peered in. "According to the schedule, this should be ready for finish work. I can't wait to see your water feature and the marble floor."

"Well, Emir suggested they set everything from the deepest point out. So they started in the hot room instead of reception. He said ultimately the stone would appreciate it more." Kyle shrugged. "I pretty much figured he knew what he was talking about."

Kyle looked uncertain, but Garrett wanted to reassure his lover that he trusted him. It was why he'd put Kyle in charge when he'd left. Granted, he'd checked in every day, but somehow this little detail had been left out. Frankly, Garrett's only concern was that they didn't need to order more supplies and completed all the chambers in the hamam within the three-week time allotment.

"Sounds like a reasonable plan. So come on already."

Garrett walked in and looked around. The contractors had only installed and mudded the greenboard drywall. He looked up and smiled at the sight of Kyle's copper bells hanging from the ceiling. They looked perfect, despite the minor panic about the installation the day before he'd left. He moved down the short corridor that led to the hot room. Eventually, as guests made their way through the hallway, which was lined in imported African ayous wood, they'd feel a continuous flow of hot air. It would help them transition from the reception area to the hot room.

The moment Garrett stepped through what would be the large, carved wooden doors, he froze. The light shining through the dome, reflecting off the honey-hued marble, made the room appear as if it had a subtle golden glow. Solid red onyx marble columns anchored the arches supporting the soaring dome. The octagon shaped *göbektaşı* rose from the floor beneath the dome, waiting for guests to lie on its heated surface and allow their worries to melt away. So far, the exterior walls were only partially tiled, but Garrett's attention was drawn to the design tiles inlaid with the marble behind the kurna because of their simple complexity.

Across the space, Emir was laying tile on the built-in bench that ran the length of the exterior wall between the *kurna* stations. The sight of his lover after a three-week absence had Garrett's feet moving across the tiled floor at a fast clip. The heels of his dress shoes clicked on the marble, which must have caught Emir's attention.

Emir looked over his shoulder and smiled. "Welcome home." He stood and started walking toward Garrett, but stopped when one of the other installers dropped his trowel.

Garrett studied Emir long and hard. His lover's coal-coloured eyes promised a proper greeting as soon as the opportunity arose. Garrett closed the distance between them and held out his hand.

"You've done a great job. How much longer do you expect it will take to finish this room?"

Emir glanced around for a moment. "We have probably another two days of tile work in here. After this, we'll lay the floor in the *soğukluk* then finish up in the dressing area. Once we lay all the tile, we'll need to come back and seal everything. We're going to do our best to stay on schedule so the finish work can begin in three weeks."

"Brilliant. I'll let you get back to it."

Emir nodded, and Garrett turned to leave. If he lingered, he knew he'd torturously tempt himself to drag Emir into the alcove and have his way with him. Garrett exited through the door leading to the cool room. Eventually, this would be where guests recovered from the heat on chaises, while being served drinks and snacks. Right now, the space was a blank slate, but Garrett knew that when they finished it, the frescos on the walls, Emir's fountain in the centre of the room, and the antique chandelier would enhance the overall experience of the guests.

"So what do you think?"

Garrett faced Kyle. "I think this is going to be the best hotel ever." He couldn't believe how much the sight of the blond-haired, blued-eyed Frenchman filled him with joy. He narrowed the distance between them. "We couldn't have done this without you."

"It's been a group effort," Kyle said while putting his arms around Garrett's waist.

"The three of us make a good team," Garrett said as he nuzzled the sensitive spot just below Kyle's earlobe.

"Mmm-hmm. In more ways than one. I want you, *mon coeur*. Want to taste you, fill you."

Garrett wanted the same thing. He knew his deadline with Edward was quickly approaching, and he'd have to sit with Kyle and Emir soon. However, Garrett wanted at least one night to enjoy their reunion.

He'd, of course, talked to both men on the phone regularly during his absence. Garrett's body stirred at the memory of the night they'd used FaceTime. Garrett had watched as Kyle and Emir had made love.

But phone sex was only so satisfying, and Garrett really needed to feel his lovers physically against him—and soon.

"It's almost five o'clock. Let's collect Emir and go home."

"I am right here, and we need to leave now before I forget propriety. My body and heart ache for you, *canim*."

Garrett whipped his head around. He hadn't even heard Emir come in the room. He was so caught up in Kyle, he'd once again forgotten that this was hardly the place for intimacy. Garrett was fairly certain none of the construction crew knew of his relationship with Kyle, and most definitely didn't know about Emir. They never touched each other affectionately outside the trailer.

He held out one hand. "I've missed you so much."

Emir looked over his shoulder, then closed the distance between them. He put his arms around Kyle and Garrett. Garrett tucked his head against Emir's shoulder and sighed. This is what he needed. The three of them, together. It really didn't matter if they were eating, talking, working, or fucking. Sharing space with his lovers made him feel complete. Of course, shagging was generally the best.

"The driver is outside. I asked him to wait because I planned on kidnapping the two of you as soon as possible."

"Let me put away my tools, then I will join you out front." Emir walked back into the hot room.

Garrett turned toward the door leading to the dressing room. "Come on. I'm craving *Köfte* for supper."

Kyle grinned. "I'll give you some tender meat... balls to taste."

He shook his head. "Be very careful. I'm a hungry man. I might just devour whatever it is you're offering."

With a gasp, Kyle practically ran out of the door. Garrett laughed and smiled as he walked past the health facility into the lobby. It looked like the rest of the crew was already gone. When he walked out of the front door, he noticed Kyle standing beside the car talking to the driver. Out of the corner of his eye, he saw Emir walk around the side of the building. He must have exited from one of the rear doors. Garrett's heart jumped as the two men stood beside each other. He really didn't want to turn down the job of a lifetime, but his job was no longer what Garrett lived for. He would find some way to keep them all together. How he was going to manage that feat, he didn't know, but between the three of them, Garrett trusted that they'd find a solution. As he'd said to Kyle, they were a good team.

Garrett put the containers from their takeaway in the rubbish bin. Since he knew there was no food in his flat, he'd called in an order to their favourite restaurant. With one source of hunger satisfied, it would soon be time to appease the other. He crossed the small kitchen and turned the tap on in the sink. The cool water quickly warmed, and Garrett rinsed their dishes.

Warmth covered his back and Garrett relaxed into Emir's arms. He sighed as Emir nibbled on the fluttering pulse point in Garrett's neck. Garrett tried very hard to remain a gentleman through their meal. He didn't want Emir and Kyle to think he only wanted to use them for sex, but Garrett's desire had been building from the moment he got off the plane in Istanbul. The anticipation of seeing the two men he loved amplified his need exponentially.

Emir turned to Garrett and walked him backward until his back met the wall in the hallway across from the kitchen. Emir slanted his mouth perfectly over Garrett's, his lover's taste so much better than any provided by some fine dining establishment. He sculpted Garrett's desire with precision as he did one of his works of art, revealing details with each touch, each kiss. Garrett grabbed Emir's back, arching against his lover as Emir pressed close. Emir rubbed his cock against Garrett's lower belly, and Garrett pumped his hips against Emir's thigh. He moaned into the consuming kiss, tilting his head farther, offering himself completely to Emir.

The sound of falling water stopped, and Garrett opened his eyes far enough to see Kyle standing at the sink, watching them. The lust in his eyes mixed with something more profound, and Garrett melted as waves of need flowed through him. He looked at Emir, reading similar emotions in his midnight eyes. His muscles clenched and his cock grew harder than he'd thought possible. He had to have them.

He sucked on Emir's bottom lip. He nibbled and licked down Emir's smooth neck. Emir gripped Garrett's hips, then he slid his hands around to grasp Garrett's arse. He lifted Garrett slightly until their erections pressed together. Emir squeezed hard, and Garrett pushed back into his lover's large hands.

"Come on, you two. There's a bed down the hall waiting for our naked bodies."

Emir backed away from Garrett then took his hand, leading him down the hallway. He reached to adjust his cock, but he just opened his trousers, using the one hand available. Kyle pulled back the drape separating the bedroom from the study area. He watched as Kyle turned on the bedside lamp and took out the lube and condoms from the basket where Garrett normally kept them.

He released a yelp as Emir pushed him back onto the mattress. His exclamation silenced when Emir came down on top of him, capturing his mouth in a kiss that made the Turk's need evident. Emir fed

Garrett hungry sounds, and his arms were like bands of steel around Garrett. Having his lover's weight on top of him again after the weeks of separation made him dizzy. Garrett tilted his head back as Emir nipped his way down to the base of Garrett's neck. Kyle's lips captured his gasp as his other lover knelt behind him and bent over.

He writhed until he could lift his arms and put them around Kyle's hips. His hands encountered smooth skin, not fabric. Warm puffs of air brushed across his chest as Emir opened Garrett's dress shirt, kissing across his chest. Garrett dug his fingers into Kyle's legs when Emir sucked hard on one of his nipples. His cock leaked as the pain and pleasure mixed, radiating from the spot where Emir's lips marked him.

He felt Emir fumbling for the zipper of his trousers and Garrett lifted his hips to aid his lover in removing the last of his clothes. This is exactly what he needed tonight—to be surrounded by his lovers on all sides.

"I want you both. Please."

Kyle rubbed Garrett's forehead and temples. "Shh, we'll take care of you."

He adjusted his position until he got an eye full of Kyle's hard cock. In that instant, Garrett knew exactly what he wanted. He twisted and turned until he faced Kyle, then took the Frenchman deep into his mouth. Kyle gripped the back of Garrett's head as he thrust deeper into Garrett's throat. Garrett loved having his mouth fucked, and he braced his weight on his hands as he bent over Kyle's lap, taking every inch willingly.

The sounds Kyle made went right to Garrett's cock, and he moaned, undoubtedly sending vibrations along Kyle's shaft. The taste of Kyle's pre-cum mixed with Garrett's saliva. He flicked his tongue against Kyle's cock, then sealed his lips tightly and sucked as hard as he could. Kyle grunted and thrust deep.

Cool gel hit Garrett's hole and a moment later, pressure grabbed his attention as Emir pushed a finger inside him. Garrett was never one for using toys when he wanked, so he knew it would take a few minutes to open him up. He tried to focus on Kyle, but Emir's fingers were driving him to distraction. He lifted off Kyle's cock, much to the man's vocal regret, then nosed his way around the low-hanging bollocks right in front of him. Garrett hissed when Emir added another finger, but a second later, he pushed back against the invasion as his body recalled the sheer pleasure of possession.

Emir's fingers withdrew and Garrett knew in just a few seconds he'd feel the broad head of Emir's cock poised at his opening. He tried to keep his body relaxed, but anticipation and eagerness had his muscles vibrating.

"Are you ready, *canim*?"

"*Evet*, please, Emir. Take me. Do anything you want to me."

Emir bent over Garrett's back and placed his lips against the rim of his ear. "I only want to love you."

Garrett's breath caught at Emir's words, then escaped in a great rush as Emir entered him. Kyle tilted Garrett's jaw up. His hands shook as he framed Garrett's jaw. Garrett opened and Kyle pushed in slowly.

Oh my God, I am going to lose my mind. Both Kyle and Emir were inside him, claiming him with every thrust. Garrett's body became their vessel for pleasure. His heart their captive. His mind was the only thing he had left, but if insanity was the only outcome of experiencing such ecstasy, Garrett would gladly make the ultimate sacrifice.

Garrett sucked harder, moving his tongue faster up and down Kyle's pistoning cock. He clenched his muscles around Emir's shaft as he fucked Garrett's arse in long, deep strokes. Garrett's arms shook from the strain of holding himself up. His cock leaked and throbbed, desperate for a touch to release the climax building inside him. Emir adjusted his angle, sliding over Garrett's gland. Garrett lifted one hand and stroked Kyle's bollocks. He slid his fingers beneath the orbs and rubbed Kyle's arsehole. Kyle's grip on Garrett's jaw tightened. And a hard thrust from Emir sent Garrett's face smashing into Kyle's groin. Kyle's cock filled his throat. Jets of cum shot from Kyle's slit.

His lover continued thrusting, and Garrett captured the last couple of volleys on his tongue, rejoicing in the taste of his lover. Kyle caressed Garrett's hair tenderly, while Emir thrust into him in a rhythmless fashion that signalled his impending orgasm. Kyle pulled out and Garrett rested his head against Kyle's thigh. He panted and pushed back into every pounding drive of Emir's cock. The width of his lover's cock stretched him in a way that made Garrett catch his breath. Emir froze deep inside him with a great cry. Garrett tried to reach for his cock, but simply didn't have the strength.

"Oh God... Oh God... Please... Help me... Somebody..."

Emir withdrew quickly, and Garrett cried out. He collapsed onto the mattress and quickly found himself being rolled over. Wet heat surrounded his cock and balls. He had no idea which set belonged to who and he didn't care. A pair of hands pushed his legs apart and Garrett whimpered. A slick tongue licked at his abused hole, soothing and arousing simultaneously. He lifted his hand to the head buried in his lap, encountering Kyle's straighter strands. Garrett couldn't hold on for one more moment. He drew his legs up, his muscles contracted throughout his body. He arched his back and gripped the sheets as his climax tore through him.

Chapter Eleven

E mir set the silver teapot on the table along with the platter of feta cheese, black and green olives, butter, honey, and jam. A pair of warm lips kissed the back of his neck and he looked to his left and saw Garrett move around to the side of the table. Garrett set down the bowl of boiled eggs and a basket of rye rolls before taking his seat. Emir pulled the chair out to sit, but before he did, his ass received a pat from Kyle as he added the plate of sliced tomatoes and cucumbers to their breakfast fare.

The three of them served their own plates. Outside the windows and the glass door leading to the terrace, Emir noticed dark clouds rolling over the city intermixed with weak rays of sunlight. The rainy season was upon them. He saw the bush on Garrett's terrace whipping in the wind. There was a tumultuous energy swirling around the city, and Emir sensed a similar energy at their table, despite the amazing night they'd shared only a few hours ago.

He lifted the teapot and poured a cup for both himself and Garrett. Kyle, despite their continued attempts to convert him, continued to prefer his espresso. He rubbed his bare feet on the carpet beneath the table. It was one of the Turkish rugs Garrett had purchased shortly after his arrival. Garrett added a couple of tomato slices to his plate while Emir eyed his men. Garrett sat across from him and Kyle to his left.

"So, as much as I love starting the day with both of you…"

Garrett sighed, then set his teacup down. "There's something I need to tell you."

Emir swallowed his olive and was happy that the piece hadn't got lodged in his throat. This did not sound like a cheerful announcement. He'd thought for sure last night that Garrett had come home to them and had been ready to confess his love, but in the light of day, maybe last night had been Garrett's way of saying farewell.

"The day I arrived in London, Edward took me to lunch. He had an announcement."

"They're not letting go of the hotel, are they? Please, no. Not after everything we've been through."

Garrett placed his hand on top of Kyle's. "Don't worry. They're very excited about the progress we've made. In fact, they're already starting promotions to build interest."

"Then what's wrong? Oh my God, you're leaving us, aren't you? But you promised…"

"I'm not leaving. I'll find some way—"

"Just tell us, *canim*. I can see the turmoil in your beautiful eyes."

"Edward wants to retire. Well, he *is* retiring, and he offered me his position."

Kyle twisted his napkin on the table and glanced at Emir out of the corner of his eye. "But that means…"

"I would be permanently based out of London. I'd still travel from time to time, but I wouldn't relocate to the construction sites like now."

"Congratulations, *canim*. This is a great honour."

Garrett's eyes showed his desire to accept the job, which broke Emir's heart, but that desire mingled with agony. Despite his lover's pain, Emir found a little joy in the moment.

"It is an honour, but your entire existence is here. Your business. Your family. Your culture." Garrett stood, then came to kneel beside Emir's chair. "I don't want to lose you."

"*Canim*, those things are not my whole existence. They are parts of me, true, but before the two of you, I was simply going through the motions. You've brought me to life. You've given me a life."

Kyle moved to stand beside Emir's chair. He held out a hand for Garrett. "We'll make this work."

Garrett stood. He tugged on Emir's hand and Emir rose. Emir put his arms around Kyle and Garrett.

"How? Are we going to split our lives between two countries? Only being together on rare occasions or holidays. If I take this job, I can't live in Turkey full-time, and I'd never ask Emir to move to London. So what can we do?"

"We'll take this one day at a time. For right now, we'll enjoy each day we have together. When do you need to give your answer?"

"Or have you already?" Kyle asked.

Garrett shook his head. "He gave me until the end of the month."

He frowned, and Kyle's jaw dropped. "That's at the end of the week."

Garrett filled the chair he'd vacated.

"I know. We didn't expect for me to be in London as long as I was, but we had to put out some fires on the Rio project."

Kyle sat on Garrett's lap and put his arms around his neck. "If you accept, will you have to leave right away?"

Relief filled him as he saw Garrett shake his head. His heart rate decreased back to a normal pattern. Garrett took his hand and squeezed. The strength in Garrett's grip conveyed his need for Emir's strength and faith in the three of them.

"No, I'll see this project out. We still have another year of work here. But, if I accept, I will have to travel back and forth to London once a month for officers' meetings. Shouldn't be gone more than a couple of days each time. Edward will phase himself out gradually, so by the time we're done here, things would be ready for me to step in full-time."

He leaned over and kissed Garrett, then Kyle. "I think you should take the job, *canim*."

"But..."

"You may not be willing to ask me to move to England, but what's stopping me from volunteering?"

"Your business? Your family?"

"I can conduct my business anywhere. I've already done pieces for projects all over the world. Much of what I do is designed and built here in my workshop, then shipped to the contractor. While I have developed an excellent reputation in the Middle East, growing my presence in Western Europe makes shrewd business sense. I already have contacts with quarries all around the globe."

Kyle stood and looked hard at Emir. "So, if you lose your workshop, how can you work?"

Emir shrugged. "I'll find another one. The true heart of my business is my knowledge, my tools and my passion for perfection."

Garrett leaned against Emir's side and closed his eyes. His lover's touch went a long way to healing the hole that had grown in his heart since his sister's wedding a couple of months ago.

"What aren't you telling us?" Garrett asked.

Emir sighed and sat in the chair Kyle had vacated. "I know my country is becoming more accepting of people like us. Many things have improved and there are several gay-friendly businesses now open in Beyoğlu, but certain things are still very traditional. There is a level of danger to living openly. While that is true for most of the world's urban areas, I feel it is greater here. Maybe it is because our culture is so rooted in our religion, a faith that vehemently opposes homosexuality. So while it may no longer be illegal to have homosexual sex here, the views of the public are far from welcoming. If I were a loyal son of Islam, I would deny my sexuality. Many say you cannot be gay and have faith, but that is another discussion."

"I've said before how strict and traditional my parents are. What I haven't told either of you is that even now they are trying to arrange a marriage for me to a woman of their choosing." Emir saw the shocked expressions on Garrett's and Kyle's faces, but before they could interrupt, he went on. "I have made it clear to them multiple times that I refuse to be coerced into such a situation, but they persist in their efforts." Kayra had to move twelve hours away to live the life she desires. Maybe it's time I do the same." He looked across at the men he loved. "I'm tired of always looking over my shoulder, guarding my words and movements so as not to reveal my biggest secret. Going with you wouldn't be a sacrifice. It would be a gift."

Kyle dropped heavily into the remaining chair. Neither man said anything. As well, Emir was having trouble reading their expressions. A first for him, and something he wasn't at all comfortable with.

Garrett took a sip of his tea, but quickly put the cup down in disdain. "It's difficult for me to find the right words. I did not know about your parents. I thought you were comfortable living quietly as you have. There's a lot of guilt filling me that I didn't recognise how much you've been struggling."

"Does this have something to do with that night you asked me to make love to you?"

He nodded. "I spent almost an hour on the phone with my father that afternoon. We will say that things did not go well."

The smile that came across Garrett's face caused the lead that had filled his veins to dissipate, and life-sustaining blood surged with hope for their future together.

"Then I guess we have a plan. I'll call Edward with my decision this afternoon. We can work out logistics in the time to come. There is one thing that still needs to be said—well, two, actually." Garrett stood and walked over and positioned himself between Emir and Kyle. "I haven't given you the most important bit of information I discovered while away."

Kyle groaned. "I'm not sure I'm up for more revelations on an empty stomach."

He looked into his *canim's* eyes and smiled. Garrett knelt in front of him and took his hands. He squeezed, waiting.

"Ben bütün kalbimle seni seviyorum."

He swallowed and cupped Garrett's cheek. Garrett's Turkish had improved, but he still sounded like a foreigner. However, the British tinted words of love were some of the most beautiful Emir had ever heard. He looked into the crystal green eyes that hypnotised him each time they locked gazes.

"And I you. You are my life."

He bent over and kissed Garrett. Their lips met in soft confirmation. He knew Garrett's taste so well, yet every time they kissed, Emir found a new depth to the flavour he craved more and more every day.

Garrett turned and put his hands on Kyle's thigh. Emir saw the tears in Kyle's blue eyes. Clearly, the man understood what had just happened. Kyle's breathing was shallow and a little quick. He placed his hand on top of Kyle's, resting on the table. Kyle quickly looked up at him, and Emir smiled.

Garrett lifted Kyle's other hand and kissed the back of it. *"Je veux passer ma vie avec vous. Vous êtes le gardien de mon cœur."*

Kyle blinked quickly and a tear tracked down his cheek. "I'll guard one half of your heart, and Emir can watch over the other. Together, we'll make sure it grows stronger every day."

"I love you," Garrett whispered.

Chapter Twelve

G arrett took a walk through the recently plastered restaurant. Today marked the one-year anniversary of his arrival in Istanbul. It was hard to believe how different his life had become in twelve months. As the new chief operating officer of Totally Five Star Hotels, his responsibilities were increasing every day. If he didn't have Kyle and Emir to come home to at night and help him relax, Garrett's hair would probably be greyer than it already was. His men were so good about making sure he ate and slept or, when necessary, stole his laptop and tablet for an evening.

Kyle had given up his flat in Gallata and move in with Garrett. It seemed wasteful to have both places when they spent all their time at Garrett's place. Emir, of course, still had his workshop and when he worked late, he usually stayed in the attached flat, but the Turk typically spent the night at Garrett's a couple of times a week. Emir's parents were still badgering him about finding a suitable spouse.

He didn't like the stress lines that seemed to grow deeper after every conversation. Emir had told them he didn't want to come out to his parents for fear of losing them, but Garrett wasn't sure how many more excuses his lover could come up with to avoid the meetings his mother and father were determined to set up. There had been several nights when Emir had spent more than an hour on the phone with his sister, talking out his frustration.

He slid a hand across the dry plaster, checking the finish the crew had completed a couple of days ago. He looked up at the dome that arched nine meters over his head above the round room. They'd chosen to go with plaster in the restaurant instead of drywall, to preserve the old world feel. As well, it worked better on the curved surface of the dome. Ultimately, they would paint the interior of the dome with stencils similar to the lobby. Additionally, they would outfit it with a rig, shaped like a geometric star, suspending light bulbs enclosed in clear globes.

He stepped through the opening of the disguised passageway surrounding the room that the wait staff would use to venture in and out of the kitchen and around the diners. Another one of Kyle's genius ideas. Not only did it make the dining room appear circular, but once everything was up and running, Garrett could really see how it would minimise the intrusion on the guests and diners. He stepped into the kitchen. Right now, it was a big empty space, but eventually top-of-the-line commercial equipment would fill it. The management team was already seeking résumés from chefs around the world.

Basic white paint covered the walls in the kitchen, but gilding in intricate blends of blue, cream, lilac and rust graced the dining area. A specialised, highly durable, anti-fatigue rubber covered the floors of the kitchen, and polished marble gleamed in the dining room. Garrett signed off on the kitchen area, giving the next crew permission to begin installation of the appliances. The men who had completed the drywall and paint next moved on to the fitness room, and the plaster crew was headed for the lobby.

He went back into the dining room and walked over to the sliding windows. The sun shone over the Bosphorus, and he wanted to breathe the spring air for a minute instead of all the smells that lingered in the construction areas. He activated the override switch and slid the large panel of glass to the side. Eventually, the window would glide electronically with the push of a button. Garrett stepped out onto the terrace. The land they'd secured provided diners and guests with views of both the Asian side of Istanbul and the great mosques of the Fatih district, depending on where someone stood.

"Hey, I've been looking all over for you."

He turned and found Kyle behind him. "Hello. What's wrong?"

Kyle smiled. "What makes you think something is wrong? Maybe I'm just craving a kiss."

He closed the distance between them, put his arms around Kyle, and kissed him softly. Garrett flicked his tongue across Kyle's closed lips and when his lover opened, he slipped inside for a brief taste. Kyle brought his arms around Garrett's neck and adjusted their bodies so they fit together. Garrett's cock filled against Kyle's. He enjoyed the pressure and the kiss for several minutes until Kyle pulled away slowly.

"Hmm, that was nice. However, I have some bad news."

Garrett smiled and shook his head. "I knew it. All right, what fire needs to be extinguished?"

"The fixtures for the Pasha suite bath came in the wrong finish."

"Oh, I thought it was something serious. We can switch them to another suite." Kyle nibbled on his lower lips and glanced to the side out of the corner of his eye. "What?"

"Well, it's not just the fixtures for the Pasha suite. It's… all the guest suites. They're single lever, deck mounted, chrome and very modern looking."

"What! I double-checked with the supplier before they shipped. We received confirmation that we were supposed to receive thirty-six, two handled, widespread, wall-mounted lavatory fittings in hammered copper!"

Kyle held up his hands. "Don't shoot the messenger. Look, we still have to finish painting and installing the flooring in the guest suites, so this shouldn't affect your schedule."

Garrett let out a long breath and activated his tablet. "I know. I just really hate it when there's a delivery cock-up because then we have to ship the wrong items back, then wait for the correct ones to arrive. Did we check all the other fittings? Showers, tubs, public washrooms, *hamam* and health facility?" he said, while looking down at his list on the screen.

"Yes, and everything else is correct, according to the checklist you gave me from the interior designer."

"Good. The items for the kitchen, laundry, and maintenance are coming from another supplier."

Garrett pulled out his phone and selected the contact for the supplier. It rang as he put the phone to his ear. He leaned into the quick kiss Kyle placed on his cheek, then watched his lover walk away. Garrett followed Kyle back inside and closed the sliding window. He wove his way through the scaffolding still erected in the centre of the room that the plaster crew had used to work in the dome. The framing would stay until after the installation of the lighting was complete.

"Waterworks Design. How may I help you?"

"This is Garrett Sloan. There was a delivery error with the shipment we received."

"I'm very sorry to hear that, sir. Let me put you in contact with your account manager."

Garrett waited as the receptionist transferred him to his inside sales representative. When he heard the man's voicemail pick up, Garrett's annoyance level increased. No matter what time he called, Garrett always had to leave a message for Jay. Garrett respected the fact that there was a significant time difference between Turkey and the United States, where Waterwork's offices and production took place, but still it would be nice to actually not have to wait for a callback for once. They could have found a supplier closer to the project, but the interior designer had fallen in love with the fixtures and everyone had admitted that they were perfect for the aesthetic of the hotel.

Garrett heard the tone for the voicemail. He left his message with a request that Jay call him back as soon as possible. He really hoped that his supplies were sitting in the warehouse and that the wrong boxes had simply been put with the rest of their shipment, not that someone had made a mistake entering the order. Each of the fittings had been custom ordered with the desired finish and carved detail on the round handles. The dark hammered copper would match the hexagon-shaped over-counter vessel sinks that, according to his schedule, should be delivered tomorrow.

After sending the contractor a message that he approved of the plasterwork, Garrett left the restaurant. He wanted to go see the shipment that came in for himself. They stored all the supplies and materials in a locked storage container in the area that would eventually become the parking lot. As he left the lobby through the front doors, Garrett shivered. It might have been March, but the temperature that day was on the cool side. Crossing the still dirt-covered ground, Garrett saw Emir exit the trailer. He waved. Emir didn't acknowledge him, and Garrett stopped. He whistled loudly and Emir jerked his dark head in his direction.

Emir started jogging over to him. Garrett took the moment to appreciate the beauty of his lover's athletic form. Last year, Garrett attended several of Emir's football matches. His lover played centre forward for a local team. This discovery thrilled Garrett because he'd really been missing his Chelsea Football Club. Garrett kept up with their success online, but there was nothing like watching a live match.

"Everything okay?" he asked as Emir reached him.

"*Evet*, I just received word that I am going to be an uncle!"

Garrett clasped Emir on the shoulder. "Congratulations. Kayra and Meriç sure didn't waste any time, did they?"

Emir smiled and shook his head. "They wanted a family right away." Emir chuckled, "Kayra says she's so sick most of the time that she's hoping it's twins and she'll only have to do this once." Emir leaned in and lowered his voice. "I must admit that I'm hoping with the announcement *Anne* and *Babba's* concentration will be on their impending grandchild instead of me."

Garrett really wanted to kiss Emir at that moment, but out in the open like this, it simply wasn't possible. When the time came for them to move to England, he would make sure they found a place to live where they wouldn't have to hide any longer. Completion of the construction was scheduled for the end of the year. The CEO was hoping to have the grand opening for the holidays. Which, if all went well, would mean that Garrett, Kyle and Emir would leave Istanbul shortly thereafter.

"What are you doing?"

Garrett rolled his eyes. "Kyle told me we received the wrong fixtures for the loos in the guest suites. I've put a call into Waterworks, but wanted to see the delivery first-hand."

"Hmm, maybe I should check the ones for the *hamam* too."

"Kyle said they were…" Garrett looked closely in Emir's eyes. "Oh… Yes, maybe you should."

They rushed across the ground. Garrett practically tripped over his feet in his effort to follow Emir's long-legged, quick pace. When they reached the storage container, Garrett fumbled with the combination lock. He cursed as he cocked up the sequence and had to start over. Finally, the lock disengaged and Garrett pulled open the doors. The moment they were inside, Emir pushed him against the wall.

Emir braced his hand near Garrett's head. The warmth of the room was nothing compared to the heat in Emir's eyes or the grip of his palm on Garrett's hip. Garrett stared at Emir, waiting. He tilted his head up, silently asking for a kiss.

Emir leaned in a few inches, stopping just before their lips touched. Garrett whimpered and tried to close the distance, but the grip on his hip tightened, holding him in place. He lifted his arms to put them around Emir's neck, only to realise that he still held his tablet. He tossed it on the pile of boxes next to them, clutched the front of Emir's shirt, and yanked him close.

Emir froze with their lips only a couple of centimetres apart. Garrett felt the warm breaths of his lover fan across his cheek and down his neck, but Emir's mouth never made contact with his skin. Garrett shifted restlessly.

"Please, love," Garrett whispered.

In the dark, Garrett felt more than saw Emir's smile.

"All you had to do was ask."

Emir brushed his lips against Garrett's. Garrett sighed and opened to allow Emir deeper access. When his lover slid his slick tongue inside, Garrett tilted his head for a better angle. He could never get enough of either of his lovers. Garrett's idea of the perfect day would be to barricade themselves inside his flat and spend the say snogging and making love. He put his arms around Emir's neck, holding tight as their kiss deepened. Emir pressed Garrett against the metal wall, which popped with their movements, the sound loud in the small space.

Emir pulled away from Garrett's mouth, making him moan in regret until he traced his skilled lips across Garrett's jaw and down his neck. His breathing hitched when Emir sucked on the throbbing pulse at the base of Garrett's neck. Garrett gripped the back of Emir's head and held him against his skin, uncaring if Emir caused a mark. His pants turned to a cry of pleasure when Emir cupped Garrett's hard cock through his jeans.

He really wanted to jump up and wrap his legs around Emir's hips, but he didn't think the thin metal wall would support them without bulging out. It wouldn't exactly be a good thing to have an arse-sized dent in the side of the company's storage container. Garrett groaned against Emir's shoulder. He rolled his hips, rubbing his cock against Emir's palm. The friction and ache of his hard flesh nearly drove him mad. Emir captured Garrett's mouth in another kiss and Garrett opened under his lover's masterful touch.

The sounds of their love echoed in the storage container, soft noises amplified by the tin can of a space. Garrett's bollocks tightened, the pressure rising with the need to find release. He jerked away from Emir's lips, gasping for air.

"I'm going to come."

Emir fell to his knees, jerking Garrett's jeans open. "You have such a gorgeous cock. I love the way it tastes when your cum slides down my throat."

"Oh, God," Garrett whined.

Emir licked across the damp, spongy crown. Garrett braced his hands on Emir's broad shoulders and he tilted his hips for more. Emir licked around the entire head, flicking his tongue against the frenulum and dipping into the slit with a moan. Emir wrapped his lips around the circumference, then began sinking slowly down Garrett's shaft. Garrett closed his eyes, and he swallowed hard, trying to hold in the shout of pleasure that threatened to erupt.

When Garrett's cock reached the opening to Emir's throat, he held his breath. With a swallow, he nudged inside the constricting heat. His hips jerked reflexively, and Garrett tried to hold still, but his body demanded more stimulation. Emir moved up and down Garrett's cock, swallowing at the base and using his agile tongue to torment Garrett across the top. Garrett tossed his head against the corrugated metal wall, his hips thrusting, his fingers digging into Emir's muscled shoulders.

Emir slid one hand beneath Garrett's sac and rubbed his fingers against the perineum, stimulating his gland from the outside. That was the last barrier, and Garrett shot volleys of seed deep into Emir's throat. Emir continued to suck him until Garrett's cock became too sensitive to stand the sensation. He tapped Emir's shoulder as a signal, and when Emir released Garrett's spent flesh from his mouth, the air on his wet skin caused Garrett to shake.

"I'll... Give me a moment..."

Emir placed a soft kiss on Garrett's exposed hip. "There is no need. I came shortly after you."

Garrett opened his eyes quickly. "Huh?"

He looked down and, since his eyes had adjusted to the dim light, he saw that Emir's thick cock hung outside his work pants, gripped in his lover's fist. The evidence of Emir's release lay on the floor between his spread knees.

"Oh, um, well... We should probably clean that up." He took a sniff as he put his cock away and refastened his jeans. "As well as air this place out. It smells like sex."

Emir stood and adjusted himself until he was fully clothed again. "One of my favourite scents."

Garrett leaned in and licked Emir's puffy lips. "Yes, but can you imagine Çetin walking in here to grab a bag of plaster to mix and catching the smell of cum?"

Emir laughed and braced his head against Garrett's shoulder. He gave Emir a hard hug before he turned to grab his tablet. A cursory peek at the outside of the boxes that contained the incorrectly shipped fixtures confirmed the contents based on the labelling.

He turned to look at Emir over his shoulder as he walked out. "Don't forget to clean up after yourself," he said, smiling.

Garrett chuckled as the sound of crude Turkish followed him out of the door. His phone signalled an incoming call, and he looked down at the screen to see Jay's number on the Caller ID.

"Back to work."

Chapter Thirteen

Garrett stood outside the entrance to the *hamam*. He traced the carvings on the thick, arched wooden door. Emir had aged the moulding around the door to perfection. Garrett almost felt as though this door was a portal to something magical. Logically, he knew it was just a door. A year ago, it was only a drawing on paper—before that, an idea in Kyle's mind. The concept of this hotel had the task of inspiring that kind of emotion in its guests.

Two days ago, the contractor let Garrett know that they had completed the installation and testing of all the fixtures. Two hours ago, the municipal inspector had given them a final approval on all work completed in zone one. He sent a text to Kyle and Emir. The three of them should experience the walk-through together. It was the first part of the hotel that was completed in its entirety. The three of them had each put blood, sweat, and tears into this building. It was far from finished, but in Garret's opinion, this marked a rounding of the corner toward home.

Kyle ran down the hall from the rear guest suites with a huge smile on his face. "Is it time?"

Behind Garrett came a low chuckle. He turned to find Emir leaning against the wall.

"You would think he hasn't spent months cursing in French every time we even said the word *hamam*."

"Tais-toi et embrasser, mon âne."

Emir pushed off the wall and took several steps toward Kyle. *"Je serais heureux de lécher chaque centimètre de votre cul magnifique."*

Kyle froze. "You've been practicing. I have to say my language sounds far sexier with a Turkish accent."

Garrett smiled. "I've been saying that for the past year. There is something about his deep, lyrical timbre that makes my cock hard at the sound of his first word."

"Maybe someday I'll see if I can make the two of you come at the sound of my voice alone, but today, we have a tour to take."

The three of them each placed a hand against the door and pushed. Garrett instructed the inspector to leave all lights and water features on so that he could give Kyle and Emir the full effect.

They entered the *camekan*, or welcome hall. The first thing that caught Garrett's gaze was Kyle's water feature falling like a gentle rain into the stone pool Emir had carved. The coloured lights hidden within the copper bells made the water appear as though each drop glowed. When each guest entered the *camekan*, an attendant would greet them and record their presence on a tablet. They would be guided to one of the private cedar dressing cubicles that lined the room. Inside each cubicle would be a pair of wooden sandals and a *peştemal*—a colorful checked cloth to be tied around the body for modesty.

"It's beautiful, Kyle. Bloody brilliant, really."

On the walls hung large iron lanterns that filled the entire room with soft light. They walked across the room toward the hall that led to the *sıcaklık*. As they stepped through an etched glass door that was specially treated for heat resistance and moisture, Garrett got his first proper look at the completed space. It was a sunny day, so beams of light came through the portals in the dome. The beams crisscrossed the *göbektaşı*. Garrett passed between two columns, beneath an arch, then he stepped up onto the centre stone platform. He knelt and traced the onyx-inlaid design Emir had constructed. The weaving lines formed some type of indeterminate shape that seduced the eyes.

Garrett looked up at the sound of running water. Kyle stood beside one of the *kurna*. He put his hand beneath the water as it fell into one of the stone basins Emir had designed. The ornate spigots complemented the marble and the chandelier that hung over the centre stone. Embedded in the plaster over each door were medallions with similar onyx designs. Kyle and Emir joined Garrett on the octagon-shaped centre stone.

Garrett put his arms around them and gave each man a kiss. "Someday I'd like to make love to both of you right here. Our skins slick with sweat from the heat. Our bodies sliding against one another, inside one another."

Kyle groaned and adjusted himself. "*Merde.*"

"Soon, *canim*. But tonight we celebrate in another way." Emir walked away and went through the matching door into the *soğukluk*.

Kyle looked over at Garrett. "I'm not sure about you, but sex is a pretty damn good way to celebrate, in my opinion."

"Hmm, especially with the two of you, but right now this marble would be freezing on our bare arses, so let's see what he has in mind."

Kyle shivered then followed Emir. Garrett turned in a circle to get the full effect of the chamber one last time. It was perfect. He heard

Emir and Kyle laughing in the *soğukluk*. Garrett smiled as he moved to join them.

When Garrett stepped through the last door, the cool room greeted him with a more intimate feel, contrasting the luxurious cavern-like design of the hot room. Luxury still oozed from its pores with the marble and mosaic floor, crystal chandelier, hand-carved fountain and private divans. While the rest of the hotel took full advantage of the views of the city and Bosphorus, the *hamam* shielded guests from the outside world, immersing them into the experience.

The showpiece of the space was an octagon-shaped mosaic with a stone basin in the centre. Smoothly cascading over the top, the water of the fountain pooled in the basin before disappearing through an invisible drain around the edge of the mosaic. The water flowed with only the slightest of sounds, the pressure low so that it almost looked like a curtain as it fell.

"What are the two of you laughing about in here?"

"Kyle said all the water in this place gave him the sudden urge to spend a penny."

Garrett chuckled. "It's a good thing you designed lavatories in both the welcome and cool rooms, then."

"*Entente*, be back shortly."

Kyle took off for the small loo at the back of the room. Garrett stood and watched the fountain, its smooth flow calming. Emir wrapped his muscular arms around Garrett's waist and he leaned back against his lover.

"I took the liberty of making the reservations at the Terrace Marmara Restaurant for this evening."

Garrett turned, smiling. "You remembered."

Emir leaned down and kissed Garrett softly. "Of course. Tonight is the one year anniversary of our first date."

Their kiss lingered, slowly. Garrett wasn't in a rush to make it hotter, rather simply enjoy the connection.

"Were we supposed to do gifts? Because I... didn't," Kyle said as he rejoined them.

Garrett turned his head but stayed in the circle of Emir's arms. He shook his head. "No. In fact, when I realised the date, I wasn't sure if I should say anything at all."

Emir frowned and walked away. "I don't understand, *canim*. I thought anniversary celebrations were worldwide—especially ones that mark a significant milestone. Have I misunderstood?"

"No, love. You have it right. The past year has been amazing and we should celebrate. I love the two of you more than my own life, but I've never been in a relationship this long. I suppose a part of me is still afraid to leave myself exposed to ridicule or disappointment if this time wasn't as significant to one or either of you."

"In Islam, we believe Allah is the creator of all things, including our actions. Belief in Allah's power, knowledge, and control of all things is one of the six articles of our faith. We have the freedom to do as we want, but we have no control over the outcome of those choices. That outcome is our destiny."

"If I believe Allah created me to be the man I am, I choose to commit my love to the two of you. Then my ultimate destiny, which is known only by Allah, will be whatever happens from day to day as I live and trust in that love." Emir turned and looked at Garrett and Kyle. "I'm not asking you to believe in my god, but I am asking you to believe in me. In us."

Kyle walked over to Emir and put his hands on Emir's upper arms. "We have spoken no vows, and I may not be very good at the everyday romantic gestures—despite the reputation of my countrymen—but I need the two of you to know without reservation that you are most important in my life. I wake each morning thankful that I have you to share my day with."

Garrett joined Kyle and Emir. "I'm sorry, Emir, if I made you doubt my commitment to our partnership. Believe me when I say that I woke this morning in your arms with the biggest of smiles as I realised it marked our one-year anniversary. Your forethought of making reservations in the same location where we started is a gift I treasure. I will find something worthy of you."

"I do not need grand gestures." He glanced at Kyle. "Or vows of forever. All I ask is that we live every day with each other in our hearts. Respect one another, and life will follow on its destined path."

"I can do that," Garrett said.

"Me too," Kyle added.

They shared a three-way kiss. Something they didn't do often, but at the moment, it felt very right. They'd started today excited about the completion of the first stage of construction, and tonight they would celebrate the first year of what Garrett hoped would be the rest of their lives.

Kyle darted through the courtyard to cut through the centre of the hotel in order to reach the restaurant faster. He'd been in London for the past month, having been called back by his firm to consult on another project he'd been working on. It wasn't as if Kyle only worked on one project at a time. It was more like three or four. The only reason he was even on site for this long was because Garrett's company had requested his presence. And since they were paying Kyle's firm some major money, Kyle had moved to the Middle East. However, Kyle continued to work and submit designs to clients remotely. Kyle only had to travel occasionally since most of his meetings could be done via video conference. The past month had been unavoidable, though. The project he'd been working on was for the British Crown and when they called, Kyle ran.

Despite the importance of the project he'd been called away on, this hotel had won Kyle's heart and he had a lot more invested in its overall success rather than just the design. It was for this reason that he was racing to see the latest stage of completion.

While he'd been away, the interior of the restaurant was finished. The workers had installed all the lighting, flooring, and painted. This marked the third zone to be finished out on the interior. The lobby, main hallways, fitness room, lounge, and business centre were the only areas left to finish. Then, of course, the interior designer and landscaper would come in and dress the place up. Garrett mentioned yesterday they had already booked guests over the holidays. That gave them a little less than three months to have everything ready. It wasn't as if they hadn't been working hard, but the crews would double their efforts to get everything finished.

Fortunately, they hadn't had any more shipping errors. And since Garrett only insisted on top crews, they'd passed all their inspections with flying colours. Kyle skidded to a stop when Emir's fountain gurgled. Emir carved the base of the fountain to look like the plants and animals found on the forest floor. He'd seen it in pieces in Emir's workshop after he finished all the carving, but this was the first time he'd seen it all put together. The pillar began with a system of roots that grew into a series of tree trunks. The carvings on the basin were weaving and interconnecting branches topped with leaves.

"Do you like it?"

Kyle whipped his head around at the sound of Emir's voice. His lover stood near the control panel for the lights and fountain. Eventually, a decorative box would conceal the controls. Garrett stepped out from behind Emir, and Kyle couldn't stop his feet from flying across the ground. He leaped into his men's arms, trusting that they would hold him. He really didn't give a shit if any of the crew saw them through the multitude of doors leading to the courtyard from around the perimeter of the hotel, but he knew Emir did. And, although his lover held him hard, his body was stiff. Kyle backed off a few feet, his heart beating hard in combination with excitement and disappointment.

"I think it's a masterpiece. Show me what else you've been up to since I left."

Garrett took his hand, which eased some of the hurt, and led him through the door. They were outside the enormous carved columns. The two and a half meters tall, hand-carved Brazilian mahogany double doors were now installed. Kyle grabbed both of the ringed handles and pulled. The doors opened much easier than their size would belie, which of course reminded him they were on the same type of hydraulic actuated assistance system as the front doors to the lobby.

He stepped through and his shoes clicked on the dark burgundy marble. He looked up and gasped at the vision high above his head. The intricate pattern of the painted dome would have taken years to complete had the painters not used pre-formed stencils and paint guns. As it was, he was sure that the layers and different colours must have given the crew migraines.

He whistled as the light rig came to life. "Oh, *c'est magnifique*," he whispered.

Garrett chuckled. "You designed it."

He shook his head. "I had a vague idea, but it was really the electrical engineers at the firm who made it possible. I bet if all the lights are out, it would look like stars in the night sky."

"That's the idea. During the day, the diners can enjoy the painted dome and natural light from the glass wall, but when darkness falls, the only light will come from candles on the tables and the lights above. So it really will look like stars over their heads."

He moved toward the wall of windows. "You know, I've been in some of the most beautiful cities in the world, but there is something about this view that makes even those pale. Why is that? It's simply a channel of water."

Garrett came over to stand next to Kyle. "It's more than that. It's one part of three. The waters of the Bosphorus, Black Sea and the Sea of Marmara all flow in and out of each other, sharing their power and shaping the world around them. In a way, it's kind of like us."

Emir put his hand on Kyle's shoulder. "Only on a slightly more significant scale."

He turned and smiled at Garrett. "Did you really just try to equate our relationship to two oceans and a strait?"

"Sounded meaningful and profound in my head. Guess it was a little ridiculous."

Kyle kissed Garrett quickly. He didn't enjoy hearing the man he loved talk down on himself. He hadn't meant his comment to sound sarcastic.

"It was absolutely ridiculous. But I appreciate the gesture."

Garrett chuckled and kissed Kyle back. "Missed you. Glad you're home."

Emir put his hands on Kyle's hips. Kyle trembled when Emir's lips touched the back of his neck. He needed to get home and make love to his men. It had been a very long month.

"Let's get out of here. I want to be buried in your snug little ass as soon as possible."

He shivered at the dark timbre of Emir's voice. Kyle gripped Garrett's shoulders a little tighter. He pushed back against Emir. "Take me home."

"Why go home when we have a whole hotel full of rooms with doors that now actually lock available to us?"

Kyle lifted his arms over his head and clutched the back of Emir's neck. Emir's hard cock pressed against his ass. "As far as I know, they don't have beds—or lube."

Garrett slid his hands beneath Kyle's shirt. He pinched and rolled Kyle's nipples, causing him to gasp and grind against Emir.

"Who needs beds?"

"And I have a packet of lube in my pocket," Emir said against his ear.

Kyle smiled. "Awfully presumptuous."

"Not really. The two of us have been marking the days until you came home, and we didn't want to wait longer than absolutely necessary to have you."

Oh, wow. Something in Kyle melted at the sound of Emir's deep, lyrical voice. His words jump-started his heart in a rhythm that beat to the tempo of his partners' names being said over and over in his mind.

"Then I guess it's a good thing I put some condoms in my pocket earlier?"

The three of them shared a laugh at how predictable they all were. But Kyle didn't let it deter him. They'd only been together for a little over a year, so he expected the honeymoon phase to last at least another thirty or forty.

"So which suite are we going to christen?"

"Whichever is closest."

Chapter Fourteen

They left the restaurant and headed toward the rear side of the hotel where the river view suites were located. Garrett took out the master key and opened the first door they came to. The three of them walked through the arched opening. This suite was pentagon-shaped and had an arched ceiling. They'd painted it a deep red and the hardwood floor was ready for a series of Turkish rugs. Outside the window wall, there was a similar view as from the terrace of the restaurant. If guests desired, they could activate the pivoting panel of the glass wall and step out onto the balcony to enjoy the fresh air.

Kyle looked over to where the sofa would be located and found a large air mattress already inflated. He turned to Garrett and raised an eyebrow.

"What?"

"We told you we've been counting the days."

He stood still as Garrett stalked him across the room. He backed toward the mattress, lifting his shirt as he went, only to come up against a firm wall of body heat. Emir enclosed Kyle's wrists in his grip, wrapping his arms around Kyle's waist.

Garrett cupped Kyle's jaw and moved in for a kiss. The outside world blurred, and all he saw were Garrett's green eyes focused on him. He held his breath, waiting for that moment when their lips would touch again. Despite the now familiar sensation, Kyle still craved Garrett's and Emir's touch like their first time together. Garrett's lips gently grazed his. He closed his eyes as time seemed to dissipate. Their mouths brushed back and forth. Behind Kyle, Emir held him securely in his arms, but the other man didn't engage Kyle in any other love play.

Their kiss seemed to go on and on, Garrett moving his slick tongue against Kyle's. Garrett's kiss was languorous, and while the three of them knew it was a precursor to sex, it didn't feel as though his lover was filling the time until their clothes came off. When Garrett lifted his head, Kyle tried to prolong the contact further, happy to continue the kiss forever.

Emir released Kyle's hands, then lifted Kyle's shirt over his head. He held it out to Garrett, who tossed it on the floor near the mattress. Garrett strode over to the installed wet bar and picked up the controller for the smart tint windows. With a click of a switch, the wall of glass became opaque, providing the three of them with complete privacy. As Garrett came back toward them, he unbuttoned his dress shirt, one button at a time, slowly revealing the smooth expanse of his chest and abdomen.

Emir kept his hands busy at Kyle's waist, unfastening his belt and trousers. Kyle aided in the effort by toeing off his shoes. Normally such disregard for his carefully chosen outfit would bother him, but getting naked with his men was far more important than the aggravation of dealing with a few wrinkles later.

He turned and helped Emir undress. The man was in his typical sturdy work attire, so they hurried their movements without regard for materials. A pair of black snug boxer-briefs really emphasised Emir's lean hips and athletic legs. Kyle licked his lips when he caught sight of Emir's thick cock already straining the material in front. He ran his hands up Emir's firm pecs and over his muscled shoulders. The dusky tone of his skin always reminded Kyle of golden honey, which, of course, made him want to lick every inch.

Emir hadn't shaved in a couple of days and the dark hair really accentuated his strong jawline. Kyle slipped his hand through the thick black strands of Emir's hair, the curls so soft against his fingers. Emir's obsidian eyes met Kyle's. How was it possible that eyes so opaque could be so expressive? He pulled Emir's head down for a kiss.

The moment their lips touched, Emir turned them and Kyle felt his feet leave the ground as he fell onto the air mattress. The firm cushion cradled their bodies as Emir devoured him. He arched his hips and wrapped his arms around Emir's back. The hunger inside him thrummed with the demand to be sated. The sharp scent of male musk filled Kyle's nose, amplifying his need further. He needed to get his damn briefs off—now!

Emir rubbed his face against Kyle's neck. He lifted Kyle's arms, pinning them over his head, then buried his nose in Kyle's armpit, which sort of tickled, but was a complete turn-on at the same time.

"You smell so good, *aşkim*."

"I bet he tastes even better," Garrett said as he sat beside them.

The makeshift bed shifted, forcing him and Emir to roll slightly toward Garrett. It was a good thing the cushion was full-sized and one of those really thick, high quality ones. It was still a tighter fit than their bed at Garrett's flat, but so much better than the floor.

"I am sure you are right, *canim*. Why don't you keep his arms where they are, and I'll find out."

He didn't move his arms when Emir let go, and Garrett took his place. He had no problem being pinned to the bed by either of his lovers. Emir had more of a dominant streak than Garrett, but Garrett knew exactly how to send Kyle soaring all on his own. Garrett bent over and sucked on one of Kyle's nipples. Emir slid off his briefs, and Kyle sighed as his cock was released from its confines. He arched his hips in anticipation of Emir's mouth around his dick.

Suddenly, Emir pushed his legs up and Kyle let out a yell as he buried his face in his ass. Holy fuck, it had been so long. Emir's wet tongue circled and pushed against Kyle's closed hole. He'd used some of his toys while away when getting off, but there was nothing quite like human flesh.

He hissed and arched his chest when Garrett bit down on one nipple. The sting distracted him from Emir's tongue for a moment. Emir held Kyle's legs up and open. Garrett kept Kyle pinned to the mattress with his busy mouth. Kyle could do nothing but close his eyes and ride the wave of pleasure created by his men.

"Baise, sent tellement incroyable."

Garrett slid his mouth up Kyle's neck to whisper in his ear, "You are incredible." He looked straight into Kyle's eyes. "I love seeing your nipples so stiff and red. Your chest glistening as your need builds higher and higher. I love having your fine blond hairs rub against my cheek as I bite and tongue your nipples."

Kyle moaned and bucked, his cock desperate for some type of stimulation. His pulse echoed in his shaft, throbbing with life. He wanted to be buried balls deep inside Garrett's tiny pucker while Emir fucked him.

He lifted his head slightly to look down at Emir, still buried between his legs. "How many… Fuck me… How many of those condoms did you say you brought?"

Emir looked up and smiled. "I didn't. You brought the condoms, remember?"

Kyle barely remembered his name. "Right… um… Pants pocket… Somebody… Oh God, Emir… Somebody get them now!"

Emir chuckled and backed off the mattress. Kyle watched for a second before he closed his eyes and a groan escaped him when Garrett swallowed his cock. Garrett swiped the flat of his tongue over the head and wrapped his lips around the shaft. Garrett bobbed his head over Kyle's groin, taking him deep, then pulling up. Shallow, shallower, then deep, deeper, and to the point when Kyle was crying out at the constriction of Garrett's throat around his cock. Everything disappeared but the wet heat surrounding him and his lover's slick tongue swirling and licking over Kyle's flesh, devouring him as if he was the best thing Garrett had ever tasted. He shivered and his balls drew up closer to his body. Garrett kept humming and bobbing his head. He was going to lose it any moment.

"Please. I can't… Not yet!"

Garrett lifted his head.

"Sorry, but I was right. You are delicious." Kyle sighed.

Emir came back to the bed, holding up two condoms and a small travel bottle of lube. He quickly sheathed Kyle's cock, then his own. Garrett stood and stripped off his briefs. Kyle saw Garrett eye Emir, and Emir nodded.

"What are you two up to?"

Garrett gestured for Kyle to scoot over. Instead, he sat up, then knelt, shifting his weight as the inflatable bed rolled slightly. Garrett got on, positioning himself on all fours. Kyle gasped at the sight of a plug buried inside Garrett's entrance. He reached out and gripped the flange on the outside, giving it an experimental tug, causing Garrett to moan and arch his back. He tugged again, watching as Garrett's body opened to allow the toy to come slightly, then Kyle pushed it back in.

"Fuck!"

"How long have you—?"

"All bloody fucking day! Now get it out and get your cock inside me before I come."

Kyle pulled on the plug once again, studying the ring of muscles at Garrett's entrance stretch as the thick base slowly came out. His eyes widened at the size. Emir grasped his cock and Kyle would have pitched forward at the sensation if his lover's arm had not come around his chest to hold him up. While Emir slicked Kyle's cock with lube, his breathing increased and his fingers tingled in anticipation of sinking inside Garrett's heat. Finally, Garrett's body released the toy. Kyle wasted no time moving behind Garrett and pushing in.

His lover's already stretched body welcomed him home in perfection. He gripped Garrett's hips as he slid inside with one smooth push. When he was as deep as he could get, Kyle tilted his hips and pushed a little harder. Their twin moans filled the air. Behind him, Emir spread some lube around Kyle's hole and slipped a finger inside. He tried to hold still inside Garrett, but his body involuntarily thrust in tiny movements.

"Just get in me, *mon coeur*."

"I will not hurt you, *aşkim*. Only a moment more and we'll all be together again."

Kyle impatiently waited as Emir fingered him open. Finally, when Kyle was about to go mad, Emir positioned Kyle so he was bent over Garrett slightly. His ass lifted, and there was the always-perfect burn when Emir pushed through the muscles guarding Kyle's channel.

"So tight, *aşkim*. So hot around me."

"Mmm-hmm, toys have nothing on you."

"Just a little more," Emir groaned.

Kyle wasn't sure if Emir was telling him or reassuring himself. He pushed back while pulling Garrett with him. Finally, Emir buried his entire length inside him. Kyle shifted, grinding against Garrett and pushing back at the same time. Emir's arms wrapped around his chest as he thrust in slow, shallow movements.

"Ah, God... So full. So tight, Garrett. You have no idea how much I needed this. Needed the two of you."

Kyle's brain short-circuited. He had trouble finding a steady rhythm between his lovers. He was so desperate to thrust as hard and deep as possible into Garrett, while simultaneously push back and have Emir's thick cock drill him until everyone cried out in completion. Emir's deep whispers made little sense, but seemed to calm the storm raging inside him.

Slowly, he established a good tempo. It seemed the two of them were content to let Kyle set the pace. Both Garrett and Emir seemed to meet him halfway, giving Kyle the best of both worlds. Fucking and being fucked. Kyle grabbed Garrett's narrow hips and drove into him. He moved deeper and faster, Emir serving as a lifeline in the storm building inside him.

"There!" Garrett yelled. "Right there, Kyle. Fuck me."

He kept that angle, rubbing over that same spot again and again, a little harder than before. Garrett's sounds filled the room and Kyle soared as he fed off the pleasure he provided for one of the men he loved. Behind him, Emir's deep grunts hit Kyle's ears. His skin tingled, and it was Kyle's turn to shout as Emir found his target. He was so close. The constricting heat of Garrett's body, the thick rod of Emir shafting him all made Kyle's head spin.

Garrett's channel rippled and fluttered around him, clenching in waves, signalling his release. He fucked Garrett through the climax and just when he thought every vein in his body was about to burst; he came. As Kyle became lost to his own orgasm, Emir continued to thrust behind him, prolonging the experience until Kyle's balls drained of every millilitre of fluid. Warm weight collapse onto his back, and from somewhere outside himself, he realised Emir was panting hard, holding Kyle as if it were their last time.

Chapter Fifteen

E mir slid into his slippers, then wandered down the hall of Garrett's flat. His lovers were still asleep, wrapped in each other's arms. Kyle's cute little snuffles, which he swore up and down were not snores, quietly mingled with Garrett's deep, even breaths. Emir, however, had been awake for over an hour after having completed his morning prayers. Sometimes he would crawl back beneath the blankets with Garrett and Kyle after Fajr, but this morning he was restless.

Fall was officially upon them again, and while the three of them typically slept in the nude, there was enough of a bite in the air that, once awake, Emir had quickly pulled on a pair of comfortable sleep pants and a T-shirt. He needed some tea.

In the quiet of the flat, the sound of a phone going off almost made him jump. Emir quickly recognised the ring tone as his and it appeared it came from the sitting area. He remembered that after they'd finished supper last night, he'd talked to Kayra, who was due to have her baby any day now.

Maybe it's time!

He ran over to the sofas and scanned the area. His phone danced across the coffee table since it was also on vibrate. Emir picked it up and looked at the caller ID. It wasn't Kayra, and disappointment filled his heart. He selected to accept the call.

"Hello, *Babba*."

"Where are you?"

Emir took the phone away from his ear and looked at the screen, as if he could see his father's face staring back at him. He didn't like the tone of his father's voice.

"Excuse me?"

"You heard me, Emir Şahin. I am standing outside your home, but you are not here. And it is an unlikely hour for you to be out running errands. I want to know where you are."

How dare he? Emir hadn't answered to his parents for his where-abouts for more years than he'd been required to.

"That is not any of your business."

Hakan blustered about respect, which only made Emir roll his eyes. This would go on for several minutes unless he put a stop to it.

"If you would stop treating me like a disobedient boy, I might share with you I stayed at a friend's house last night," he said, loudly.

There was silence on the other end of the phone. Emir heard some rustling sounds from the bedroom. He must have spoken louder than he realised. He peered down the hall and saw Garrett sitting up in bed, looking at him worriedly. Emir waved him off, gesturing him to lie back down. He blew Garrett a kiss then headed for the terrace doors. As he stepped out onto the balcony, he shivered. It was colder than he'd suspected, probably hovering somewhere around twelve degrees, but the sky was also cloudy so there was little sunshine to warm his bare skin.

"Who is this friend?"

"His name is Garrett. We were working late last night and he offered me a place to stay."

He silently apologised to Garrett for the lie, but didn't have a choice.

"You work with this man. Is he another labourer at the hotel? I thought the hotel was being built in Beyoğlu. There is hardly reasonable living near there. Certainly not something a tradesman could afford. Why would you travel to his man's home and not yours?"

Emir clenched his jaw. His father had never seen him as anything more than skilled labour. Emir had tried to explain until he was blue in the face that he, as a respected business owner and artisan, made a very comfortable income. Too set in his ways, Hakan refused to see past Emir's rough hands.

"Garrett is technically my boss on the hotel project, but we are also friends. He has an apartment in Cihangir."

"You should not be mixing socially with management, Emir. I've told you it is not appropriate many times before. Why do you not listen to me?"

"Because I don't agree with you."

Emir had never understood his father's views on that topic. It was almost as if he clung to the class system of years past. It wasn't even that his father looked down on people who worked as tradesmen. Hakan had worked in a manufacturing plant for a power management company for almost forty years. But he did firmly believe that a man should not behave or associate with those above him.

"Father, it is seven o'clock on a Saturday morning. Why are you calling me? Better yet, why are you standing outside my home?"

"I came to discuss the necessity for you to end this unacceptable behaviour with taking a wife. You are far past the age when it is appropriate to disregard your responsibilities."

Emir sighed. He pinched the bridge of his nose and closed his eyes. And the morning had started out so peacefully. He jerked as something heavy settled over his shoulders. Looking back, he saw Garrett standing behind him. His lover had placed a blanket around him to ward off the cool morning air. Garrett smiled, bent over and kissed Emir's forehead. Garrett mouthed 'Love you', then went back inside. Emir couldn't stop the tear that gathered in the corner of his eye and threatened to fall.

"I have told you repeatedly that I have no desire to marry at this point in my life. Why do you keep pushing the issue?"

"Because you are the last Şahin male. It's your responsibility to ensure that our family name lives on. Your sister has already done her duty by Meriç's family—or she will shortly."

It almost made Emir sick to hear his father call his soon-to-be-born grandchild a duty instead of the miracle all new life represented. He also knew damn well that if Kayra and Meriç heard their father speak like that, they'd make sure Hakan would never have the chance to influence their child.

"They abolished the sultanate in 1922. We are not *Osmanlı Hanedanı*. So other than ego, why are you so desperate that I produce some type of heir? Why are you convinced I should live my life according to your dictates?"

"Because I am tired of hearing talk that my son is *kahrolası bir ibne*!"

Emir gasped. He'd never heard his father use such vulgar language. There were a couple of different ways to deal with this situation. He could simply hang up on his father, but Emir had never been actively disrespectful to either of his parents. He could tell the truth once and for all and confirm his sexuality, if not for the offensive term his father had used. Or he could, as he always had, deflect.

"You do not deny that you are one of those disgusting, unholy perverts?" Hakan screamed.

"I have no intention of responding to vulgarity. If you would like to sit and speak like men, then you know how to reach me. However, as I have said before, my life is my own, and I expect you to respect reasonable boundaries. That includes not demanding entrance to my home at an early hour without an invitation."

Emir waited for a response from his father. He heard the other man breathing heavily through the phone. He lifted the phone away from his ear and was about to hang up when his father's voice came out of the speaker.

"Meet me at the Yedi Tepe Kafeterya near our home in one hour."

His father hung up and Emir let out a sigh of relief he hadn't realised he'd been holding. His mother and father lived in the Altunizade neighbourhood on the Asian side of the city. In fact, if Emir walked to the end of Garrett's terrace and looked across the Bosphorus up into the hills, he'd be looking right at the area where he'd grown up. Standing, he stretched his arms over his head. He did not know what he was going to say to his father in an hour, but right now, he needed to go inside and kiss the men he loved. He needed Kyle's strength and Garrett's compassion to fill his soul before he had to face any more vitriol from the man responsible for helping to give him life.

Emir opened the door leading to the salon and found Garrett and Kyle snuggling on the sofa. They both turned to look at him with questioning expressions. Emir closed the door and then walked over to them. He knelt on the floor at their feet and laid his head over their legs where they pressed together. Two hands rubbed over his back, neck, and shoulders.

"Is there anything we can do, *mon cheri*?"

Emir slowly shook his head. "I need to get dressed and leave. My father has commanded my presence in an hour."

Garrett tilted Emir's face up with a finger under his chin. "Do you want us to go with you?"

"*Hayir*, this is something that I need to do alone. I have a feeling this meeting will decide whether I still have a family."

Kyle bent over and kissed Emir softly on the lips. "You will always have a family. Kayra will not turn her back on you, and we have each other. You met my parents last year and they love you. I think you talk to Garrett's parents more than he does," Kyle said, smiling. "If your father can't accept you for who you are, then it's his loss."

"My head knows you're right, but my heart hurts for the loss of my *babba*."

"He may surprise you," Garrett said.

Emir blinked to hold back the tears threatening to escape. "You didn't hear the things he just said to me. My father has always been stern, but never hateful. Not toward me."

Kyle slid to the floor beside Emir and wrapped his arms around him. He soaked up Kyle's strength. Warmth flowed over him from behind as Garrett joined them on the floor. If things went as he expected, then he only had to survive another few months in the city.

The three of them were already working on plans for the move to England. He had contacted another local artisan to see if the man wanted to buy out Emir's stock and workshop. They were currently in negotiations for the sale. His tools would go with him. He'd spent years collecting the pieces he preferred and would ship them to England. Fortunately, Emir didn't have a great deal of personal possessions he had to pack and ship. Clothes, some treasures from his childhood—photos, collectibles—but all his furnishings would stay with the apartment.

Emir nuzzled into Kyle's and Garrett's embrace for a few more seconds then got up off the floor. He gave each man a kiss before walking down the hall toward the toilet. He'd take a fast shower before leaving. Emir had taken to keeping a couple of changes of clothes in the apartment, so at least he wouldn't have to wear his work gear.

He took a deep breath then opened the door to the coffeehouse. The scents of tea and strong Turkish coffee hit him. A shot of caffeine might have settled his nerves, but Emir didn't think his stomach could handle anything taking up residence. He turned his head to the right and left, searching for his father. Emir saw him sitting at a table in the corner, but he wasn't alone.

Emir quickly crossed the room. When he got to the table, he stood, eyeing both his parents. "*Anne*? Why are you here?"

"Because your father and I would like to talk to you."

Hakan opened his mouth, but one swift look from his mother kept one of the most opinionated men Emir knew quiet as a lamb. Emir glanced around and saw an empty chair at a table two over. Since the table was unoccupied, he took the chair and brought it back over to where his parents sat. Emir sat and peered back and forth between them, waiting for someone to break the silence.

"Your father has something he would like to say."

Emir stiffened. God, could he really hear those hateful words again? In such a public place? The coffeehouse was mostly empty, but it simply made little sense that his father, who was a very private man, wanted to confront Emir in such a public place.

"I want to apologise for the way I spoke earlier. I was—I am... upset. But that does not—"

"Hakan!"

Emir's father cleared his throat. His fingers turned white as he gripped his tea cup.

"Tell us about your work. Is the hotel nearing completion?"

So it appeared that they were going with the avoidance route. Just like always. Well, fine. Emir had been doing this dance for twenty years. "Yes. We should complete all the finish work by the end of this month. Next month, all the staff will go through training. I have only a few more pieces to install in the lobby area, then my portion will be complete. The grand opening event will take place in December. You can be my guests, if you'd like?"

"We will consider it," Hakan said.

Emir nodded. There wasn't much to be said after that.

"And what project will you do next, son? Another hotel?"

He wished he had that tea now, so he could fiddle with the cup. "I'm not starting another contract. In fact, I'm moving."

Rana frowned. "I don't understand. You're moving your workshop? I thought you liked the old fire station?"

"It's not my workshop that I'm moving. It's myself."

His father's face turned even stonier, if that were possible. His mother appeared to examine her cup of tea. She spun it slowly on the saucer, but when she cast her eyes up toward Emir, the raw pain in them almost made him say he'd take it back. However, he wouldn't turn his back on Garrett, Kyle, and the life they wanted to build together.

"Why do all my children leave me?" Rana asked, softly.

"*Anne*, we're not leaving you. You raised us to have strength and intelligence. Kayra and I are both living the lives we've created for ourselves from the lessons you taught us. We're happy and successful adults. *You* made that possible. These should not be sad times but ones filled with happiness."

Rana covered Emir's hand with her own. "My head knows you are right, but my heart hurts for the loss of my babies. Will you be joining Kayra in Adana? The two of you always shared a special connection. It would make me feel better knowing she had family close with the baby coming any day."

Hearing the same words he'd said to his partners come from his mother made Emir realise that regardless of the distance between them or the status of their relationship, he would always carry those who'd taught him the meaning of love from the cradle in his heart.

Emir squeezed his mother's hand, took a deep breath then let it out slowly. "I'm moving to England."

"England!" Hakan shouted. "That man—your boss—is from there. It's true, isn't it? You are a faggot. You're *his* faggot!"

The last remaining patron stood and quickly left the teahouse. The worker behind the counter seemed to have disappeared too—a fact that Emir appreciated. Emir didn't respond verbally, but he knew the moment that both his parents read the truth in his eyes.

"You are a man without dignity! I will never allow you to enter my home again!"

Rana stood quickly. "Hakan, you will stop—"

Hakan turned toward Rana. "Sit, wife! You had your turn to talk, and now it is mine. Allah forbids such acts. You are an unholy abomination. I will see you banned from every mosque in the city."

Emir saw the manager of the coffeehouse start in their direction, but he shook him off. He was leaving. He'd said what needed to be said, and as much as his father's words had cut deeper than a knife straight through his heart, Emir accepted he was not responsible for the man's words or his opinion. If Emir's father would ever accept him, then it had to come from within his heart. Emir could not forcibly change his mind or plead for understanding because any acquiescence from such actions would be false.

He reached out to give his mom, who had tears running down her face, one last hug, but his father pushed his arms away.

"You will not touch my wife with your unclean hands!"

Emir stood tall and gazed into his father's eyes. It was funny. He had never realised until that moment that he was actually taller than his father. "I will always love you, *Babba*."

Emir turned and left the coffeehouse. He made it about one block before his legs gave out on him. Fortunately, he'd unconsciously wandered into the park where he used to play as a boy. He saw a young boy running around a grove of trees, his sister chasing him. Emir's heart clenched in longing for Kayra's warm smile and trembled in fear for the little boy who had lost the innocence that filled his days with laughter.

He wasn't sure how long he sat there, but slowly the sounds of the children playing and the light faded. The coldness of the stone bench seeped through his jeans, but it didn't faze Emir, as his insides were already frozen. A presence crowded him and he tried to focus through the fog rolling through his mind.

He looked on either side of him. "How did you...?"

Garrett put his arm around Emir's shoulders. "We figured out where your parents lived and have been searching the area for hours."

"And now we're going to take you home," Kyle said.

Emir stood and let Garrett and Kyle lead him away. The sound and meaning of the word home had transformed in the last ten hours. Emir wasn't sure what 'home' would mean to him in the future, but for now, it was a haven where he could be himself with the men he loved.

Chapter Sixteen

The hotel was finished. Garrett stood outside, looking at the exterior. The copper roof gleamed, despite the overcast skies. In fact, maybe it was his fanciful imagination, but he thought the copper was like a beacon drawing guests from worldwide. The warm colour of the reclaimed brick made the building seem authentic, instead of a flashy start-up. The landscaping team had finished dressing the grounds a few days ago. There were gently sloping green areas, trees with several years' worth of growth, bushes and rocks. The stone laid parking lot curved in front of the front entrance under a portico held up by four of Emir's carved limestone columns.

"You designed an amazing place, Kyle," Garrett said.

"And you ensured the build matched his design," Emir added.

Kyle stepped up between them. He turned to Emir. "And you brought it to life with your amazing artistry. Without your skills, this would have been just another chain hotel with a fancy name."

Garrett started toward the entrance. The soft opening event would begin tomorrow night. Everything was in place. Their jobs were done. But tonight he had one last surprise for his men.

"Let's take one last inspection."

The three of them walked up the stone-laid path. The moment they came close to the massive carved wooden doors, the portals swung open smoothly. When they entered the lobby, Garrett immediately lifted his eyes to the iron and crystal chandelier that hung from the centre of the dome. The Turkish carpet runway, which had been custom woven, led guests straight to the reception area. Garrett, Kyle, and Emir followed the path.

He reached the front desk and smiled at Leyla. They selected her as reception management because she spoke five different languages. Since they were expecting many international travellers from both the business and leisure sects, they wanted each guest to feel as comfortable as possible. Leyla and two other multilingual employees would be available for interpretation in any capacity throughout the hotel if needed, day or night.

"Hello, sir. Are you checking in?"

Garrett smiled and played along. "Yes, my name is Garrett Sloan. I believe you have a reservation?"

Leyla tapped on the screen of the computer system, then looked up at the threesome. "Yes. I see that you have the Pasha suite reserved and have requested a dinner reservation upon check-in. The bellman will arrange for your luggage to be brought to your suite, and Orhan will give you a tour of the amenities available on your way to the restaurant. Please enjoy your stay and let us know how we may be of service."

Leyla pushed a button on the console and seconds later, Orhan, one of the concierge agents, joined them from his post not far away. The designers created the system with a handheld electronic paging system that was part of the employees' uniform, allowing any employee to contact another. All Totally Five Star hotels used them, and to date, it was a much more efficient and consistent method of communication than telecommunication to a station.

"Gentlemen, please follow me."

He saw Kyle and Emir smile at each other as they rolled their eyes. He knew this was staged, but he wanted all the employees to feel comfortable in their roles before proper guests arrived tomorrow. Granted, there was only a skeleton staff on hand tonight, but he'd done what he could. The day and night managers, as well as all the employees, had undergone a month's worth of training, but Garrett had seen first-hand what happened when practice ended and it was game time.

Orhan gave a very eloquent and friendly description of the lounge area, the business centre. He pointed out the entrances to the court-yard and could even explain some of the architectural elements when Kyle and Emir got into the spirit and asked the young man some questions.

They reached the restaurant and Garrett got a little nervous. He knew Emir and Kyle probably were expecting another show, but Garrett had arranged for the chef to serve the three of them a private five-course dinner. If all went as planned, then the moment they opened the massive carved doors, his men would be treated to an evening of decadence and enchantment. Garrett sent up a brief prayer.

Orhan opened the door, and Garrett let Kyle and Emir walk in before him. Kyle gasped as he entered. The clear crackle glass single bulb shades of the large light structure glowed softly. The muted colours of twilight hung low in the sky outside the wall of glass. All the tables and booths would have full service to prepare for tomorrow's event. As per Garrett's instructions, every tea light at the centre of the tables flickered softly in their coloured globes. To finish setting the ambience, soft folk music played from the invisible sound system.

"Garrett? What is all this?"

"This is our night. During the grand opening, we'll be busy entertaining guests. I wanted to give the three of us one night to enjoy the fruits of our labour. So we're having dinner, then a reservation for full service massages in the *hamam*."

Emir smiled and Garrett saw him wink before he sat at the table Orhan indicated was theirs. It was situated under the center of the dome. He held out a chair for Kyle. Orhan's eyes widened slightly, but Garrett didn't care. In two weeks, the three of them would be several countries away, living the life they chose.

Kyle joined Garrett and Emir, but before he sat, he gave Garrett a quick kiss on the cheek. "Thank you."

Orhan had agreed to be their server for the evening. So he efficiently—and, much to Garrett's approval, with complete professionalism—brought out the bottle of wine Garrett had pre-selected.

"Tonight the chef has prepared a five course meal. There is a tapas plate as an appetiser. You can choose from prosciutto, julienne cut salami, roast beef and an assortment of cheeses. We also have figs, pitted dates and peaches to accompany your selections. The second course will be a romaine salad with cherry tomatoes and an olive oil and balsamic vinaigrette dressing. The soup prepared is a creamy celeriac, and your entrée is grilled, yogurt-marinated lamb shoulder chops with braised vegetables. Finally, for dessert, the chef has a special treat for you—a decadent chocolate mousse."

Kyle groaned. "Oh, my... I'm not going to be able to move after this."

Emir and Garrett chuckled. Garrett nodded to Orhan in thanks. The man quietly left. Garrett put his hands on the tabletop with his palms up. Both Kyle and Emir put their hands in Garrett's and he gave them a squeeze.

"Good surprise?"

Emir leaned over and kissed Garrett. "You are a treasure. I can't believe you went to all this trouble. How did you get the staff to agree to come in tonight just for us?"

"Being the chief operating officer of the corporation that writes their paychecks has some benefits."

Orhan placed the appetiser platter in the centre of the table. Garrett took a piece of prosciutto and rolled it together with some smoked Gouda cheese and an olive in the middle. He held it out to Kyle. Kyle leaned forward and opened his mouth expectantly. Garrett fed him a bite and shifted in his seat when Kyle moaned as he slowly chewed. He turned to look at Emir and smiled when Emir held out a soft date for him. Garrett accepted the piece of fruit. The sweet flavour burst over his tongue.

Kyle fed Emir a peach, and Emir's eyes flared. He sucked in a breath when Emir allowed his mouth to linger, sucking on Kyle's fingers. They continued to feed one another with various selections. Garrett saved the beef for Emir, since Muslims do not eat pork. The chef had originally wanted to serve scallops, but Kyle had a shellfish allergy. The last thing Garrett wanted for his romantic dinner was an evening spent in the hospital with a partner in anaphylactic shock.

Orhan appeared with the next course moments after they'd finished the last bite. He must have been monitoring them, but Garrett hadn't felt as though they were being observed. In fact, despite the large room they occupied alone, the atmosphere felt very intimate.

Kyle followed Garrett and Emir through the courtyard. That afternoon, they'd had a rare snow. It was only deep enough to reach his ankles, enough to make everything outside look pretty and get his feet wet if he wasn't careful. Probably by morning it would all be gone, simply a memory, but Kyle thought tonight it made the courtyard a little more magical. The sound of Emir's fountain trickling gently enhanced the feeling. There was a subtle glow from the small white lights highlighting the pillars of the verandah on all sides of the courtyard.

At the moment, there were only some bare trees, low bushes, and topiaries in the space, but come spring and summer flowers would fill the courtyard. The gardeners strategically placed stone benches and wooden swings so the guests could linger and enjoy the garden. The plan involved hosting a cocktail hour once a week with live music, where roaming servers would serve guests drinks and appetisers.

They stepped onto the verandah on the other side and Emir opened one of the arched glass and wood doors. They stepped directly into the hall outside the door leading to the *camekan* of the *hamam*. There had been a lot of debate regarding the type of door and signage that should be used. Kyle had originally intended for the entrance to have a glass door so guests could peek in as they walked past, luring them to use the services. But during one of the design development phases, the board of directors had vetoed the concept. Kyle had to admit that the door did look fantastic. They ultimately had the word '*hamam*' carved into the door instead of posting a different sign.

Emir opened the much-debated door and Garrett and he followed him into the reception room. He smiled as he saw the belled water feature running. He kept looking around so much that he didn't notice their greeter until he heard her voice.

"Good evening, gentlemen. If you follow me, I'll show you to your individual dressing rooms. Inside you'll find the *peştemal* and sandals for your use. Please disrobe to your comfort level, but keep in mind that your attendant will give you both a full body scrub and a massage."

He entered his cedar dressing cubicle. It wasn't a large space. Approximately the size of an accessible changing room. He quickly stripped to nothing, hanging his clothing on the hangers and a rod above the built-in bench. He wrapped the chequered cloth around his waist like a towel and slipped on the wooden sandals. Kyle slid open the small door and stepped out. He heard the soft slide of a door to his left and saw Emir dressed identically to him. Kyle admired Emir's physique, as he did every chance he got. Garrett joined them a moment later. The three of them followed the attendant through the heated hall and into the hot room.

"I'll leave the three of you to relax and soak up the heat. As soon as your muscles loosen and you've had a chance to build up a sweat, we'll be back to begin your services."

Kyle went through the arches and headed right for the *göbektaşı*. The marble floor that Emir had worked so hard to install was warm beneath his feet. He already felt his body letting go of the stress that always lingered in his muscles. He stepped up onto the centre stone and stopped when he was directly beneath the apex of the dome. Since it was now dark, no light shone through the portals. Instead, the interior was lit with several sconces. He lay down on the stone and put his arms behind his head, looking up at the dome he'd designed.

Garrett reclined beside Kyle. "You look bloody hot," he said, turning his head toward him.

Kyle smiled and looked over at Garrett. "Not yet, but I'm getting there."

Emir relaxed on the other side of Kyle. "I'd be happy to help you along. If I slide my hand through that slit, will I find your bare cock? Could I stroke the velvety soft skin and feel it harden in my grip?"

"If you get to play with his cock, then I want to suck on those tiny brown nipples. I can already see sweat blooming over his smooth chest. Makes me want to lick it away and trace my tongue over every inch of his tight stomach."

Kyle moaned and squirmed. "The two of you are evil fuckers. There is no way I can hide a hard-on in this scrap of fabric."

Twin chuckles reached him from either side. Kyle closed his eyes and drifted. His partners were now silent. He'd been in Turkey for almost two years and yet this was the first time he'd experienced a *hamam*. One part of him was upset because this felt amazing, and he knew that some of the historical *hamams* in the city were spectacular both from an architectural standpoint and because of their reputation for services offered. However, he also felt as though this experience was even more special because Kyle was in a space he'd designed.

He turned over on the stone and sighed as the heated surface touched the bare skin of his chest. He was working up a good sweat, his body releasing all the toxins and purifying itself naturally. A hand rubbed his right calf and another his left arm. Kyle smiled. He loved that Garrett and Emir wanted contact with him whenever they could get it. Ever since Emir had come out to his parents, he'd seemed more relaxed. Exposing the secret he'd held for half his life had seemed to release an invisible burden on Emir's soul. He knew Emir was upset about the discord that now existed with his parents, but Kayra had called right away and made sure her brother knew she stood beside him. Kyle had hoped that someday the rift in the Şahin family would heal.

"It's time for your baths, gentlemen."

He slowly opened his eyes and looked up at the three *tellaks* who stood beside the *göbektaşı*. He blinked a few times. On his right, Emir gave his shoulder a squeeze then moved to the side of the stone. Kyle looked over at Garrett who shifted over to the opposite side.

"Sir?"

Kyle sat up and saw the third *tellak* waiting for him at the edge of the stone, down by his feet. He scooted toward him while trying to maintain his dignity.

"Please turn sideways and lie on your back."

Kyle followed the *tellak's* instructions. Warm water poured over him, soaking his skin and the cloth. It was a good thing that his erection had disappeared, otherwise the thin fabric would have left nothing to the attendant's imagination. The young man used a foam sponge to cover him in white frothy suds. The massage that followed had Kyle groaning. His muscles and joints popped, which he couldn't help but grimace at, but a sigh of pleasure followed it. After a thorough rinse, Kyle's *tellak* led him to one of the raised marble tables near a *kurna*.

The *tellak* scrubbed every inch of his skin with kese, a natural exfoliate. As layers of hidden dirt and dead skin fell away, Kyle could actually feel his skin breathe. Afterward, they treated him to another soapy wash and rinse with warm water drawn from the kurna.

"We have finished. If you would like, you may join your friends on the *göbektaşı* for some final relaxation before adjourning to the *soğukluk* for recovery."

Kyle returned to the centre stone and waited for Garrett and Emir to finish their scrubs. It wasn't long before they joined him once again. Kyle looked around and noticed that the *tellaks* had disappeared.

"I arranged for Erol, Kivanç and Zeki to be the last to vacate the hotel. We are now officially alone." Garrett let his *peştemal* fall open, and he spread his legs. "I believe Emir made us a promise."

Chapter Seventeen

G arrett opened his *peştemal,* leaving his body completely nude. The sight of his lover reaching between his legs to grip his semi-hard shaft left Kyle momentarily enthralled. The flesh got harder and harder, his eyes following each stroke of Garrett's hand. Emir came into Kyle's line of sight, also naked. He knelt beside Garrett. Both their bodies were still slick with water and the heat of the room made the atmosphere hazy with moisture. It was as if he were watching a live action dream.

Emir took over for Garrett's hand. He caressed Garrett's cheek, and Kyle felt the echo of the rough, callused skin against his own. He loved how every touch made them feel alive.

"You are so perfect, *canim,*" Emir whispered.

The way Emir gazed at Garrett as he slowly stroked their lover's cock reminded Kyle of how a person studies a great work of art in a museum or how he probably looked staring at a building designed by one of the greats. Garrett sat up. Emir straddled Garrett's lap and pulled him straight into his arms. Emir closed his mouth over Garrett's. With every touch of his lovers' lips, it felt as though the air was stolen from his lungs, his heart beat so wildly that he feared it would explode from his chest, and his blood rushed so quickly through his veins his skin felt hypersensitive.

Kyle noticed his breathing had increased. He wanted nothing more than to walk over there and experience those soft lips stroke back and forth against his. He craved Garrett's gentle tongue teasing the seam of his mouth and Emir's powerful arms wrapped around him. Garrett opened his mouth to Emir's questing tongue. Their lover pressed deep into Garrett's mouth. Kyle's feet moved of their own volition. Every cell that his scrub and massage had awakened called to feel his lovers' bodies against him.

He dropped his wrap and stepped up behind Emir. He slipped his hands into wet, dark, silky hair. Kyle's cock throbbed. Hot. He wanted to rut against Emir's broad, muscled back as his lover undulated over Garrett. He thought about dropping to his knees and sucking Emir, maybe even trying to get both men's cocks in his mouth at once. God, that would be hot. Sucking both his partners until their eyes rolled up into the backs of their heads. Emir's body draped over his. Garrett's thrusting up from the floor. Or maybe Emir could ride Garrett and Kyle could fuck Emir's mouth? Then again, he enjoyed being the middle man too. So many choices!

Emir released Garrett's mouth. He looked up and back at Kyle. "I was wondering how long it would take you to join us."

"I was enjoying the show."

He caressed the side of Emir's smooth jaw. The dark eyes looking up at him filled with love and heat. He bent over and kissed his Turkish heart. Emir slid his soft, wet tongue against Kyle's lips and he opened in welcome. The moment he sensed an opportunity, he drove inside Emir's mouth. How the man always tasted so fucking good, Kyle had yet to figure out. Their kiss was long and lustful. Kyle tried to put all his desire for a lifetime of love into each caress of their tongues.

Emir pulled away, but Kyle didn't let go of the back of his head. He turned and kissed Garrett, allowing their flavours to mingle. Garrett's lips were warm, soft, sweet. The three of them kept trading off. Each kiss was deeper, more intense. Kyle's cock ached at the sight of Emir devouring Garrett. As Emir turned toward him, Kyle could no longer tell the difference in their respective tastes. They'd become one. The ultimate aphrodisiac. Their tongues, cocks, and bodies pressed together. At some point, they'd lain down on the stone with Kyle in the middle. Garrett and Emir kissed over top of him, and the perfect opportunity arose to take things to the next level.

He reached for both men's cocks, one in each hand, and stroked. Twin moans blended above his head. Kyle's strokes faltered as both his lovers gripped him. When Garrett's and Emir's mouths separated, only to follow parallel paths down Kyle's chest and stomach, he thought he'd died and gone to heaven. Garrett licked one side of Kyle's cock and Emir on the other. The two men moved up and down Kyle's length. He pushed his hips into each caress, moaning and muttering his lovers' names over and over. He gripped the back of Emir's and Garrett's heads, holding them over his throbbing flesh.

Kyle looked down his body to watch Emir and Garrett share a sloppy kiss around his cock, which was nearly his undoing.

"Arrêter! Je ne veux pas venir."

Emir chuckled as he rested his chin on Kyle's stomach. *"Ben bizim musluklar hem doldurmak istiyorum."*

Kyle frowned, blinking away the fog of lust. "Huh?"

Emir dropped kisses all along Kyle's hip bones as he said softly, "I said I want to fill you with both our cocks." He looked up into Kyle's eyes. "Then we can fuck you until you scream with pleasure."

Oh... my... God. Was such a thing even possible? Kyle vaguely remembered seeing a porno once with double penetration and there were guys who enjoyed fisting, so he supposed if all parties were patient and relaxed enough, it was possible. Did he want that? While the physical idea was a little nerve-racking, the concept of having both Emir and Garrett inside his ass at the same time seemed like the ultimate way to share their love and intimacy. There was just one problem.

"What about stuff?"

Garrett knelt beside Kyle and held up a glass bottle. "This is a very special lube. I placed it on the table of oils and perfumes earlier to prepare for tonight. Not only is it ultra-long lasting, but it also has special ingredients to relax the muscles."

Kyle stared at the coloured cut glass. He hadn't even been aware that Garrett had left their little body pile. Garrett tipped the bottle and squeezed. He knelt beside Kyle, waiting. Kyle let out a slow breath and nodded.

Garrett hesitated. "If you don't want this, say so. Because if not, I'm more than willing to take your place. The idea of both you and Emir stuffing me senseless is an ultimate fantasy."

Kyle shook his head. "I want this. I want to feel you both." Kyle pulled his legs back. He gripped behind his knees to hold himself open for his partners.

Garrett smeared the lube around Kyle's hole. He always loved the first touch of his lovers' fingers tracing his opening, and when Garrett slid a finger inside him, he sighed. His body welcomed the intrusion. One finger quickly became two. The lube was good. Slick. Smelled pleasant. And Kyle could tell that whatever special ingredients were inside actually helped his body relax for what was coming.

Kyle moaned when Emir added two fingers to Garrett's. His body stretched. His cock leaked. Soon Garrett's and Emir's fingers weren't enough. Kyle needed something thicker, longer. He needed his lovers' cocks.

"How?" he gasped. "How are we going to…?"

"Garrett, lie down, then Kyle, you straddle him."

Kyle climbed over Garrett. He bent over and kissed his sweetheart. He held Garrett's cock as he adjusted to find the right angle. The head kissed his hole, and he paused, enjoying the anticipation of having Garrett inside him. Kyle lowered his hips slowly. Since they'd done away with condoms, the sensation of merging their bodies was so much stronger. The first time he'd slid inside Garrett without a barrier had nearly caused Kyle to lose his mind. With Garrett inside him, Kyle raised a little, then pressed down, hard.

"Bloody hell!"

Kyle made good use of the muscles he worked hard to achieve in the gym. He rode Garrett as if the devil himself were chasing him. With his hands braced on Garrett's chest, he raised and lowered himself over the man's long cock, convinced that his lover had reached new depths inside his body. He halted his movements when Emir rested his large hands on his shoulders, settling him down on Garrett's cock. Garrett thrust upward as he pulled Kyle down onto his cock.

Emir wrapped an arm around Kyle's waist and bent over him. Out of the corner of Kyle's eye, he saw Emir's strong thighs bulge as he strained his muscles to hold the position. Kyle felt more pressure against his already filled hole. In maddeningly slow increments, Emir pushed his way into Kyle's body. He'd never felt so full in his life. At first, there was a flaring bite of pain, but it quickly morphed into a burn that consumed him with pleasure.

The look of ecstasy on Garrett's face clued Kyle in to the fact that it must feel pretty good to have their balls pressed together and their cocks rubbing, as Emir thrust. Behind him, Emir moved faster, tightening his arm around Kyle's waist. Emir's breath in his ear and dark words in Turkish had Kyle crying out.

"Oh, mon dieu! Si plein! Si bon. Ne cessez pas de me baiser!"

"Never thought anything could feel so good," Garrett moaned.

Beneath him, Garrett's hips thrust in small increments, almost as if it was involuntary. Emir was the driver, and Kyle wished this journey would never end. He licked his lips, as they were dry from him, panting and moaning. He opened his eyes to look down at Garrett.

"You have got to try this, *mon cheri*. It's like nothing else in the world."

"Feels fucking amazing from down here, too."

Emir upped the pace, and Kyle tilted his head back to look up at the dome high overhead. He cried out as Garrett took hold of his cock and jacked him off. *Oh, fuck yes!* Garrett's hand pulling, Emir's cock pumping, two cocks stretching him to a near breaking point. He was going to fly apart into a million pieces. Emir pulled Kyle's head back and claimed his mouth.

A flash of light exploded behind his eyes, a bolt of lightning arced down his spine, and Kyle came in a rush of fluid that made him lightheaded. Beneath him, Garrett moaned long and low, his head thrashing on their marble bed. Emir's hips punched into Kyle until he let out a warrior's cry. Kyle felt the moment a torrent of cum flooded his ass from both his lovers.

They collapsed in a heap on the heated stone surface. Emir's chest rose and fell in great heaves. He took Garrett's hand and pulled him up behind him. Kyle scooted them over until his head lay in the crook of Emir's shoulder. He sighed as Emir kissed his forehead, the simple act almost more poignant than the rigorous acrobatics they'd completed. They lay together while their heart rates returned to normal.

Kyle felt as though he needed another scrub at this point, but he wouldn't have given up this experience for anything. Garrett rolled away from them, but not before Kyle felt a kiss warm the back of his shoulder. Now that the lust had burned off, the heat of the room was getting to him.

"I've brought some water to rinse us off."

Kyle peered over his shoulder and smiled at Garrett, standing at the edge of the stone. When Garrett poured the water over his body, Kyle moaned at the refreshing coolness. By the time Garrett finished cleansing him with the water, Kyle felt as renewed as he had after his scrub from the tellaks earlier.

The three of them walked hand in hand to the cool room after cleaning up the *sıcaklık*. The air hit Kyle's bare skin, causing him to shiver.

"There are some drinks and fruit on the counter over here. Why don't we relax for a little while, then we can go to the room and get a good night's sleep."

Kyle put his hand on the back of Garrett's neck, then pulled him in for a long kiss. Emir angled so their kiss became a three-way.

"I love you, *mon cheri*," Kyle said softly. He looked at Emir *"Ve sen benim Türk kalp vardır."*

Emir smiled, *"Je chéris ton amour."*

Kyle wandered through the grand opening reception being held in the lobby. The cocktail hour was in full swing, but because of the number of people and the cool weather, only a few brave souls were outside in the courtyard. The restaurant would serve meals until well into the evening. They'd initially considered having more of a banquet type setting, but the owners wanted all the guests to experience the hotel as they would as guests, so each person received an appointed reservation for dinner upon his or her check-in.

He had just finished giving a tour to some businessmen from Paris, and now was hunting for a glass of wine and maybe a quiet corner to soak up the atmosphere. While he enjoyed a pleasant party occasionally, he was generally better at one-on-one or small groups.

"Kyle LaFleure! There you are, you genius!"

He turned to see Cybil Proulx, one partner at his architecture firm. He put on his meet-and-greet smile, then sauntered over to her.

"Cybil, lovely to see you. So glad you made the trip for the event."

"I wouldn't have missed it for anything. This place is a masterpiece. You can guarantee the firm will submit for awards for both the building and you. You have a dazzling future, young man."

"*Merci*, this project has pushed me to think beyond convention. I wanted to do justice to this amazing city and its history, while still providing all the luxury and conveniences today's discriminating travellers expect."

"Well, you have most definitely succeeded. I heard a disturbing rumour that Totally Five Star has offered you a very lucrative opportunity to work for them full-time."

"They did, but I've already turned them down. I don't want to only design hotels. One thing I enjoy about working at Wilkinson is the versatility of the projects we contract."

"Good answer. And don't be surprised if they use the term 'partner candidate' for you within a couple of years if you continue producing quality work like this."

While it was very gratifying to hear that he had a promising future at his firm, for Kyle, his real goal was to design spaces that called to people's souls. If he could accomplish that, then the project was a success. It just so happened that this project was designed based on the yearnings of his own soul. And the miracle was that his soul had found its mates in the men who had helped to make his dream come true.

Emir wove his way through the crowd, mingling in the lobby. As far as he could tell, operations with the soft opening were going well. Everywhere he looked, people wandered around with their heads tilted upward. There were several languages overlapping one another from the different guests. He couldn't understand them all, but the ones he could kept exclaiming over the beauty of the dome.

Emir saw a flash of blond move across the room. He would recognise Kyle anywhere. A woman dripping with diamonds caught his lover. Emir recognised Kyle's polite smile, the one he frequently wore when he did video conferences with clients. He turned and saw Garrett at the opposite side of the room talking to Edward, his mentor and the man he was replacing on the board of directors.

Everyone who'd been lucky enough to get reservations for this weekend had received dinner reservations and complimentary drinks and hors d'oeuvres during the cocktail hour. Management had brought out the heat lamps for the courtyard because there was still a bit of a bite in the air, even though the snow had already melted. Emir was really there to support Garrett and Kyle. Nobody knew it was his stonework and fountains throughout their luxury hotel. And truthfully, Emir didn't mind the obscurity. It was enough to hear the admiration as guests and dignitaries walked through the halls and commented on how elegant everything looked.

It was hard for him to say which piece he was proud of more. As with every project he took on, he put his heart and soul into even the smallest of details. Certainly, the most challenging was probably the twelve foot tall carved columns outside the restaurant, but the piece that would serve as the cornerstone in his memories was the fountain in the courtyard.

He didn't know if Kyle or Garrett had noticed the patterns of the carving, but everything was done in threes. Three tree trunks, all with three branches that sprouted three limbs, intersecting as they led up to the leafy top. For Emir, it was a monument to their time here in the city he called home before home became the two men who held his heart.

"Emir?"

He turned around quickly at the sound of the hesitant, soft voice. "*Anne*? What are you doing here?" He looked around for his father, but when he felt a soft touch on his arm, he focused again on the small woman in front of him.

"He's not here. I was hoping your invitation to the event was still open. I would very much like to see what you have been up to these last many months."

Emir pulled his mother into his arms. "You are always welcome—wherever I am."

"Will you give me a tour? I've heard wonderful things since the moment I walked through the door. This lobby is very impressive. If it's an example of what to expect throughout, then you have built something very special."

"That's very nice of you, Mother. But I only helped with the window dressing. The genius of the project is the man standing just over there," Emir said, pointing in Kyle's direction. "And that man," he said, pointing to Garrett next, "made sure it was actually built."

"And he is your... The man who...?"

"He is my partner. In fact, both of them are."

Rana gasped and looked around. "Please. I am not ready to discuss such things. I don't understand your desires, nor do I approve. As a woman of faith, I believe what you are doing is wrong. But you are my son and I will always love you. As you have said many times, you have your own life to live. I did my best to give you a proper foundation, but you are responsible for your own choices. I will pray that you accept Allah in your heart once again."

Emir didn't want to start a fight here. And while he didn't agree with what his mother had said, the fact that she was here at all meant everything to him. It gave him hope that they might have some kind of relationship again.

"Let me show you around," Emir said, holding out his arm.

A firm grip on his arm halted him before he moved even a single pace. He looked down at his mother. Had she changed her mind?

"I know your father gives you a lot of grief about your work, but I want you to know that I've always been very proud of you. You are an artist and a successful businessman. I've made inquiries through acquaintances and they have informed me you are extremely sought after in your field. You have a reputation for excellent quality and fair prices. I'm sure you'll be a success in England."

Tears prickled the backs of his eyes as his heart ached with love for his mother. "Thank you" were the only words he got out, despite his desire to say everything in his heart.

Garrett kept one eye and ear on Edward and the other on Emir across the room. He noticed Emir stiffen the moment he turned around and saw the small woman in the *hijab*. He suspected that the woman was Emir's mother. While Garrett hoped that the two of them could find their way together again, he wasn't about to let his guard down. It had taken him and Kyle days to bring Emir around after his confrontation with his parents a couple of months ago.

"Son, this place you've built is first class all the way. You should be very proud of what you have accomplished here."

Garrett focused once again on his friend, mentor, and colleague. "I am proud. I think this is the best hotel we've ever built. And I personally believe it wouldn't have been possible without Kyle's and Emir's talents."

"I agree with you. I've heard rumours about the fact that Emir Şahin will be relocating to the United Kingdom. You wouldn't know anything about that, would you?"

"Since when did you pay attention to gossip?"

"Since one of my best friends told me he's in a relationship with two other men—one of whom he met when I sent him to Turkey on a job assignment."

Garrett chuckled and glanced around for another look at Kyle and Emir.

"Of course, there is the fact that you can't seem to keep your eyes off him and LaFleure for more than five minutes."

"All right. Yes. Emir is moving to London when Kyle and I return. He's going to re-open his business once he finds the right space."

Edward rubbed his hands together. "Perfect. This is going to make luring him in so much easier."

Garrett arched an eyebrow. "What are you talking about?"

"I've been talking with the other board members and we'd like to offer Emir a retainer position. This hotel is going to serve as our new flagship. We want someone with his talents on call for each successive new project."

Garrett looked over to where Emir had been, but his partner had walked away. Garrett didn't see the woman Emir had been speaking with, either.

"You, of course, are welcome to ask, but I don't think Emir likes being tied to a single organization. That's why he opened his own business. He's very selective about the projects he takes on."

"Hmm, well, we will see. We are prepared to offer him a generous contracting fee. And he would still be available to take on whatever private projects he desires."

"As long as they don't inhibit the progress of Totally Five Star business."

"Would you try to dissuade him from our offer? I thought this would make you happy? I thought you enjoyed working with him?"

"I would never speak against the company, but Emir shouldn't feel pressure to accept a position because of my allegiance. I've loved working with him and Kyle, but I know this scale of this project is not typically something he does. We were extraordinarily fortunate that he agreed. Besides, since this was my last on-site project, it's a kind of moot point. If you think of logistics, we build all over the world. Some locations will not have the space or access to materials as we did here in Istanbul. What do you expect him to do? Ship a five-ton column of stone halfway around the world? Maybe a better use of his talents would be utilising his contacts in masonry and art to cultivate local artisans if the project called for it. This hotel called for a lot of stonework, but many of our properties won't have any. It will all depend on the location."

"Bugger, I hate it when you make a better point than I do."

He put his hand on Edward's shoulder and squeezed. "Don't despair. I was due for one, eventually. You've had the upper hand on me for years."

Edward sighed. "Guess I'm getting addle-brained in my old age. Good thing I'm retiring."

He scoffed. "Retiring is a relative word when it comes to you, my friend."

"I am what I am. Although, my dear wife has threatened to do me bodily harm if I don't take her on that extended vacation I've been promising for the last thirty years. So you'll have at least a couple of months without me looking over your shoulder."

Garrett chuckled and held up his glass of champagne. "To another successful project?"

"To a successful project, good friends and—bloody hell, I'm feeling sentimental—to true love." Edward raised his glass.

With a clink, the toast was sealed.

Epilogue

Emir put his key in the lock of the front door. Kyle pressed his warm lips against his neck, causing Emir to moan and stall in the process of getting the door open. Kyle wrapped his arms around Emir's waist and played with the buttons on the front of Emir's shirt. Their lover always got a little more amorous after a few glasses of wine. Emir had been half-heartedly fending off his touches the entire taxi ride home from the restaurant. His breathing got a little shallower, and he leaned back against Kyle. When Kyle licked the pounding pulse point at the base of his neck, Emir couldn't hold back a moan.

"Hey, you two. Let's take this inside," Garrett said, standing behind them.

He opened his eyes and tried to focus on the small piece of brass. All he had to do was turn the key, open the door, and walk through the opening. Yet with Kyle's hands and mouth doing wickedly delicious things to his body, Emir was having a hard time—in more ways than one.

Garrett pushed Emir and Kyle to the side. "Bugger it all, I'll do it myself."

He turned and embraced Kyle. He took Kyle's mouth in a kiss that had the man pressing hard against him. Kyle backed him up against the brick beside the door, and it was Emir's turn to grip his partner harder and thrust against him.

A sudden jerk caused him to open his eyes. Garrett had a hold of his arm and yanked him through the door. Kyle chuckled and followed closely behind him. They made it halfway down the entrance hallway before Emir pinned Garrett to the wall.

Emir moved in for a kiss, but right before his lips touched Garrett's, he diverted and nibbled on his partner's sensitive jawline. "What's the matter? Afraid we'll get the bobbies called on us?"

Garrett gripped the belt loops of Emir's trousers. "No, I— Oh, God that feels good."

"Yes. You taste delicious." Emir backed away from Garrett's neck and gave a brief peck to his lips. "Now I have something to show the two of you."

He walked down the hall. He passed the door to their bedroom and looked over his shoulder to see Kyle and Garrett standing outside their room with questioning looks.

"Um, *mon coeur*? This is where the magic happens?"

He smiled. "Really? Because I seem to remember some pretty magical things happening in the reception room, kitchen, garden and, let's see... How about the night we all—?"

"Okay, point made. But where are you going now?" Kyle asked.

"I said I have something to show you. I promise we will pick up where we left off in a few minutes. But for now, follow me."

He turned left and made his way through the furniture of the main living room. They'd left the pendants in the kitchen on, providing him with enough illumination to avoid running into the sofa or the tiled coffee table. Emir glanced over his shoulder and saw Kyle and Garrett following behind him. He smiled at them, crooked his finger, then resumed his trek. As he looked out of the windows and glass doors on the far wall, he noticed the small path lights glowing softly around the ground level decking of their private garden.

He opened both doors and walked outside. His eyes immediately went to the surprise he'd made for his men, and excitement filled him. Earlier in the day, he'd brought home the fountain he'd been working on since he'd reopened his business. It had been important to him to have the fountain here when they got home from their dinner since today marked their three year anniversary.

Getting the four foot wide granite base through the front door had been a tight fit, but with some patience, tenacity and luck, he'd been able to manoeuvre his gift through the doorframe. The granite fountain featured three levels. Emir designed it with the appearance of three rocks being split in half and then stacked on top of each other. He'd left the exterior with its rough natural finish and polished the top of each layer smooth.

As he stepped onto the patio, he heard the telltale bubbling and tinkling of water. Emir turned to his left to see the fountain working. Water came up from the centre of the top stone and flowed smoothly over each tier. As he'd instructed the installers, the base rock sat on a layer of river rock.

"Oh, my God! How did you...?"

"I brought it home earlier and hired a crew to install it while you were at work. The message I got in the middle of dinner was them informing me they'd finished the job."

Garrett put his arm around Emir's waist while Kyle stood in front of him. Emir pulled Kyle back against him. The three of them stood and watched the fountain. Emir had fashioned tiny lights to sit in the crevice between the different layers of rock, so the entire display had a soft glow in the dark.

"It looks beautiful, love." Garrett said.

"*Oui*, a perfect complement to our home. I love the natural rock. While I'm constantly in awe of your more formal limestone creations, this garden needed something less ostentatious. A big basin and carved piece wouldn't have looked right."

"I see you continued your theme of three."

He smiled and gave Garrett a kiss on his cheek. "I wasn't sure if you ever noticed that. For this piece, I thought it even more appropriate. The three of us are celebrating three years together." He turned toward his partners and got down on one knee. He took Kyle's and Garrett's hands. "I love the two of you a little more each day we share our lives. While I know the world will never legally acknowledge our relationship, I kneel before you tonight to ask if you would do me the honour of becoming my husbands, even if it's only in our hearts."

He looked up at his partners, anxious for their responses. Three rings had been burning a hole in his pocket all night.

Kyle nodded silently. He cleared his throat and swallowed. "Yes," he whispered.

Garrett squeezed Emir's hand and smiled. "Absolutely."

He let out a long breath and bowed his head. He stood, then reached into the pocket of his lounge jacket. "Good. Then I can give you these." He opened the extra-large box that held all three rings.

Kyle slowly reached out and removed one. Emir had found a design that had a unique three-strand braid in a satin finish. The overall effect looked like three ribbons layered over and around each other.

"That one should be Garrett's, if I got my sizing right."

Kyle turned to Emir and held out the band to him. "You should put it on. You're the one who proposed."

He took the tri-coloured circle and looked at Garrett. Garrett held out his hand, and Emir noticed it had a slight tremor. He took Garrett's hand once again, instantly stilling the shake. Emir slid the symbol of their love partially onto Garrett's left ring finger. He took Kyle's out of the box and slid it on partially. "Garrett and Kyle, tonight I ask to join your lives. I pledge to be true to you, to respect you and to grow with you throughout the years. We are many things to each other, and I will strive only to have those best qualities continue to shine. I pray our bond continues to grow stronger. Time may pass, fortune may smile, trials may come, but no matter what we may encounter, I vow here tonight that our love will be my only love. I will make my home in your heart from this day forward."

Emir slid the bands on his partners' fingers completely. He leaned in and kissed Garrett, then Kyle. Emir tried to keep the kisses brief, but the moment his lips touched those of the men who had changed his life and opened his heart, he found it very difficult to pull away.

"Hey, what about you?"

He held out the box.

Kyle lifted the remaining circle. He looked at Garrett. "Together?"

He held out his hand, and when Kyle and Garrett slid the piece of jewellery on his finger, he felt something in his heart lock. Shortly after they had begun their relationship, he made a commitment to his men. But tonight, as Garrett and Kyle slid the piece of jewellery on his finger, he felt the last thread of his heart irrevocably woven with their acceptance of his vow.

Garrett took Kyle's hand, and Kyle took Emir's. The three of them walked back into the flat and Garrett led them to their bedroom. The room was dark until Garrett turned on one of the bedside lamps.

Time seemed to slow as the three of them removed one another's clothes. They didn't rush the effort. They never seemed to get far before someone stopped the progress with a kiss or a touch.

He reached the point where he had only his trousers remaining. Garrett reached for the fastening and when his fingertips brushed over Emir's skin, he sucked in his stomach. Their eyes locked as Garrett unfastened the button and inched the zipper down. His full cock pressed against the fabric, and when Garrett cupped him through his briefs, he reached out for Garrett's shoulders and steadied himself.

Garrett dropped to his knees and removed Emir's trousers completely. He opened his mouth and sucked Emir's cock deep. Emir held onto the back of Garrett's head, not forcing but cradling as Garrett used his talents to start Emir on his journey to finding the ultimate pleasure. Kyle came up beside Emir and held out his naked cock. His new husband released Emir and took Kyle into his mouth. He blessed the sex gods that his lover enjoyed sucking cock as much as he did. It was not as if Emir or Kyle would ever complain, unless, of course, Garrett stopped.

This time Garrett got both him and Kyle worked up enough to where he thrust hard, pushing into his mouth, then Garrett would disappear and switch partners. It was both maddening and fucking hot watching Garrett suck on Kyle's cock. They'd made love countless times over the past three years, but something about tonight made it feel new all over again.

Garrett stood, and Emir dragged him up against him in a hard kiss. He grabbed Garrett's bare ass and played with the trench, causing Garrett to shiver and moan. It was so much fun to turn the tables. Over Garrett's shoulder, Emir spied Kyle climb up on the bed and lie on his back. He turned Garrett around so they could both look at the vision waiting for them.

"Isn't he beautiful?" Emir said softly in Garrett's ear.

"Mmm-hmm, I love to watch him jack that long cock, especially when it's already slick and shiny from my mouth."

Kyle closed his eyes, tilting his head back and following Garrett's indirect command. He spread his legs a little wider, and Emir's gaze was drawn to the curves of Kyle's ass.

"I like to watch him finger himself," Emir said.

"Oh, yes, that's always an amazing sight," Garrett said, nodding.

Kyle slipped two fingers into his mouth. They came out dripping with saliva, and Emir tightened his arms around Garrett as Kyle pushed them through the ring of muscle guarding his channel. He watched as Kyle slid his elegant fingers inside, then pushed down to take them deeper. Emir knew exactly how it felt to be inside that hot, velvety tunnel. Garrett left the circle of Emir's arms and walked around to the other side of the bed.

Kyle's pale skin, highlighted by the soft glow of the lamp, beckoned Emir toward him. He climbed up on the bed and pulled Kyle's fingers out of his ass. He draped his body over Kyle's. Emir combed his fingers through the blond strands and looked down into Kyle's blue eyes. If Emir ever had any doubt about what Kyle was feeling, all he had to do was look into the eyes that matched a summer sky and he'd have his answers. Tonight they reflected all the love Emir held in his heart. Emir wasn't sure exactly what he wanted to do first, but he knew the one thing that always made Kyle let out a bunch of happy whimpers.

He leaned down and kissed Kyle while he played with the small, sensitive nipples on Kyle's chest. Kyle responded as expected and wiggled around until he spread his legs, cradling Emir between his thighs. Kyle's talented mouth had Emir moaning his own tune of pleasure.

"Who wants to be in the middle?" Garrett asked.

He didn't stop kissing Kyle as he raised his hand. He felt Kyle's response to the question throbbing against his stomach, and when he opened his eyes and peered over his shoulder, he saw Garret's hand up, too. Emir chuckled as he scooted down Kyle's stomach, laying kisses along the flat plain.

"It appears we have a three-way."

Kyle snorted as he laughed, causing Emir to roll his eyes.

"Not that kind of three-way. Well, actually, yes that kind of three-way, but not what I meant," he chided.

Garrett and Kyle were full out laughing at this point.

"Oh, shut it! Both of you!"

"So what do we do? Draw straws?" Garrett asked.

Kyle lifted his head with a glimmer in his eye. "Measure dicks?"

He rolled off Kyle and lay back on the bed with his hands behind his head. "I suggest the two of you figure it out. I'm going to lie here and ogle your naked bodies while I fantasise about filling my mouth with your cocks."

He wrapped his hand around his cock and gave it a slow, hard tug. Garrett's dick bounced with excitement. Emir's flesh was already hard and with each stroke of his fist, the blood rushed to his cock faster and faster. Kyle and Garrett shared a look, and Emir let out a mental cheer.

"Ready for a Turkish smorgasbord, *mon cheri*?"

He smiled and tried to look innocent. "Me?"

Garrett knelt on the bed and crawled over to Emir's other side. He put his arm around Emir's waist and purred against his neck. "Like you weren't angling for this? But that's okay. I can't wait to get you between us, make you lose the power of speech."

He groaned as Kyle took hold of his cock, and Garrett pinched his nipples. He closed his eyes when the edges of his vision blurred. The last time he had been in the middle, not only did he emit animalistic roars, but he almost lost consciousness.

Kyle bent over and swallowed Emir's cock. He sucked in a harsh breath, gripped the sheet, and thrust up his hips. "Gah..."

"Already working. We're good."

He shook his head, opened his eyes and cupped Kyle's cheek. "You're the best."

He received a nuzzle from Kyle. Kyle kissed the tri-coloured band that now encircled Emir's left ring finger. He turned to look at Garrett. Green eyes smouldered with hunger. Garrett traced Emir's lower lip with his thumb. He nipped at the pad of Garrett's digit. Garrett pressed his thumb into Emir's mouth and Emir sucked on it. He watched Garrett's pupils blow wide.

"*Mon Dieu*, the two of you are stunning together," Kyle said.

He pulled Kyle down on top of him. He loved the feeling of his lovers' weight on top of him. Kyle took a kiss that had Emir's toes curling. By the time Kyle was done, Emir was breathless, rocking their hips together.

His cock was so hard he wasn't entirely sure he was going to last long enough to be in the middle of anything. Kyle was making hungry, needy noises, moving against him hard and fast, cock painting a trail along his stomach. Garrett was hardly a casual observer. He rubbed his hand along Emir's right side. He glided his fingers over the skin just above Emir's hip, that always made him shiver. Garrett's hot mouth worked at Emir's neck, drawing his own needy noises out.

He wasn't sure when Kyle had managed to conjure up the lube, but it became apparent that he somehow had when he felt slippery fingers slide over his ass and down as far as his balls.

"*Aman Tanrım*," he groaned. "I need you inside me. It's been forever."

"Yes, too long," Garrett said in his ear. "We're going to make you feel so good."

Then Kyle pushed his fingers into him. Garrett pulled one knee farther to the side, spreading Emir's legs a little wider. He pushed back onto Kyle's hand, unable and unwilling to stop.

Emir blindly searched for Garrett's hand. He needed an anchor for the storm brewing inside him as Kyle probed and stretched his body. Kyle kissed his way down Emir's chest. He took Emir's cock in his mouth, causing him to cry out in Turkish. The last time he'd allowed his mind the freedom to immerse itself in his lover's touch, it had left Emir feeling the echoes of the experience for days afterward. Already, he sensed that tonight would be just as transcendent.

Allowing Garrett and Kyle control over his body, experiencing their love for him made him feel powerful, strong and needed. Kyle lifted one of Emir's legs and straddled the other. He was about to ask Kyle what he should do when he felt the head of Kyle's cock pushing at his hole.

"Oh... More."

Kyle pushed until his entire length filled Emir. The pressure and fullness inside him were unlike any other. Kyle began to thrust, slowly. He withdrew his cock only to spear Emir again and again, picking up the pace with every lunge. Emir gripped Kyle's leg, the soft hair tickling his palm. It was funny... The tiny details the brain cataloged as shut down. Emir opened his eyes wide enough to see Garrett smiling down at him. Garrett tapped Kyle on the shoulder and Kyle pulled out.

"No!" Emir shouted.

Garrett brushed aside the strands of Emir's hair that had fallen over his forehead. "Shh, it's okay. I promise we're going to send you to the stars."

Garrett moved to straddle Emir's head. That put his cock right above Emir's mouth, which he quickly took advantage of. Emir sucked the tip of Garrett between his lips. Garrett wrapped his arms around Emir's thighs and pulled both of them back, opening him once again for Kyle's cock. Kyle drove inside with one hard thrust that had Emir screaming in pleasure all over Garrett's steel-hard flesh. Wet heat surrounded his dick. Uniting their bodies as one sent Emir to another plane of ecstasy.

Kyle moved in him, hands on the backs of his legs, using the leverage to drive deep inside with long strokes. He would have told his men how good everything felt, how his heart and body felt so full to bursting, but Garrett was fucking his mouth in a way that had Emir clutching the curves of his ass and moaning as saliva dribbled out of the corner of his mouth.

Their thrusts left Emir helpless to their demands, his body their symphony to conduct. After a few moments, it seemed as though Garrett and Emir picked up on Kyle's pace. Their rhythms synchronised and sensations washed over Emir like a windstorm, one pressure leading to the next and back again.

"Take him, *mon coeur*. Take his ass and make our proper Brit scream around your fat cock."

Kyle's deep, husky voice hypnotised Emir into following his commands. Emir felt around for the lube. He got some out and on his fingers, all the while sucking on the cock being driven into his mouth. Emir's breath came in hitching gasps as Garrett pushed faster and faster. Emir didn't waste any time pressing a finger into Garrett's hole, because he knew in only a matter of moments, he was going to come so hard his brain could not sustain higher function. He unerringly found Garrett's gland and massaged until the sweet flavour of his husband's pre-cum flowed onto his tongue.

He couldn't do much moving on his own with Garrett above him and Kyle slamming into him, but he hardly felt passive in their love. Emir rocked with Kyle's and Garrett's movements. Judging by the sounds his lovers made, the small amount of extra stimulation forced their orgasms to loom closer.

Kyle's murmured French spurred them on, making up for the fact that both Emir and Garrett had their mouths full. While Emir was partial to his native language, he could definitely understand why many considered French the language of love. Hearing Kyle's deep voice in that lyrical tongue was very effective in making Emir's blood rush faster, his cock drip more and his balls tighten with the need for release. It didn't matter what the words were or the fact that he understood only a handful of them. Kyle's thrusts were smooth and strong, his cock rubbing over Emir's prostate with each drive of his hips.

As he added another finger to Garrett's channel, he moaned and grunted around Emir's cock. His only wish was that he could look into the eyes of the men he loved with all his heart as their bodies gave in to the ecstasy thrumming through them. When Emir had the chance to look into Garrett's and Kyle's eyes as they came, it was as if he had a direct line to their souls.

Garrett stiffened, his cock pressed deep into Emir's throat and the warm wash of Garrett's cum spilled into him. Emir massaged Garrett's gland as the man rode out his orgasm, the vibration around his cock as Garrett screamed, sending Emir hurtling toward his own climax. As soon as Garrett's cock softened, he released the flesh, arched his head back and came with a roar, letting loose all the sounds he hadn't been able to before. Kyle used his arms as manacles around Emir's legs, and he felt Kyle's cock throb with release deep inside his ass. His lovers had marked and claimed him in a way just as intimate and meaningful as the way Emir had claimed them in their private garden ceremony.

As their heart rates and breathing slowed, Emir pulled Kyle and Garrett up against him. The three of them cuddled in a pile on the bed where they would share their love, in the home where they would share their lives. He felt the pull of sleep tugging at him. It was the end of one day, and Emir looked forward to the dawn of many more to come.

Connect with Trina

- Website: www.trinalane.com

- Subscribe to my newsletter

- Email: trina@trinalane.com

- Facebook: trina.lane.books

- Facebook Group: Trina's Tantalizing Tales

- Instagram: trina.lane.books

Leave a Review

Thank you so much for reading Turkish Delights. If you enjoyed this story, please leave a review to tell other readers how much you loved these characters. Sharing your reading experience with others on retailers and social media helps people find new reads and supports indie authors.

Thank you,

Trina Lane

Other Books by Trina

Got Your Six Series

Zero Control

Northern Currents

Thunder in the Skies

Dreaming Color Series

In Dreams He Came

WaterColors

The Heart of Texas Series

Shards in the Sun

Windows in the Mist

Phantom River Series

Scent of Seduction

Only A Mate's Touch

Taste of Devotion

Sound of Salvation

<u>Perfect Love Series</u>

The Perfect Balance

The Perfect Union

His Perfect Partner

Capturing Perfection

Simply Perfection

An Imperfect Reunion

<u>Stand Alone Novels</u>

Turkish Delights

Taking the Chance

Love's Return

About Trina

Trina is a scientist with a passion for history, music, and photography. She loves to travel and experience new places but is terminally shy around people she doesn't know. When the zombie apocalypse occurs, you'll want to find her because she's a crack shot, and promises to take out those nasty decomposing flesh-eating vermin before they have a chance to make you their snack. Her favorite aunt gave Trina a sultry romance novel to read while they were on vacation together back when Trina was in middle school and made her promise not to tell her mother. She's been hooked ever sense! Her choices in reading and writing material are as diverse as her Apple Music library, which contains music from Mozart to Metallica. Her one concession is all stories must have a happily ever after ending—did we mention she's incurably romantic? She's the mother of a very strong-willed and sweet young man who frequently makes her smile and grimace within seconds of each other. She firmly believes that the sweetness comes from her, and the other part is her husband's fault. She loves to hear from readers and her greatest wish is that we all strive to achieve bigger dreams.